The Other Side: The Reveal

By O'Jay Barr

Above the
BARR PUBLISHING

Copyright © 2021, O'Jay Barr

Cover image: ©

ISBN-13:978-1-7372584-0-7

Publisher's Note

Although the author and publisher have made every effort to ensure the accuracy and completeness of information contained in this book, we assume no responsibility for errors, inaccuracies, omissions, or any inconsistency herein. Neither the publisher nor the author shall be liable for damages arising from here.

DEDICATION

This book is dedicated to all the amazing women in my life. During my journey of writing this book, I realized I am surrounded by a crew of badass women! So to my wife, my daughters, my granddaughter, my mother, my grandmother, my sister, my aunts, my cousins, my sister-friends and every other woman in my circle - thank you for inspiring and supporting me. This is for you, keep pushing, I see you and I love you!

1. JOSEPHINE

"Did you have a good time tonight?"

"I did." I smiled down at Sadie standing in the doorway.

"Are you going to call me?"

"I don't know."

"Oh, that's how it is?"

"You know exactly how it is. You knew that before you got here."

"Yeah, I know. I was just hoping-"

"Look, sweetheart, you know how this works. I call, you come, we cum, and that's it. I can't give you more than that. So, if you're looking for more, next time, I'll have to call someone else."

"No, no, I'm not looking for more. I'm okay with the arrangement. I was just hoping you might call sooner," she said, pouting her full lips.

"Hmmm, good night Sadie." I kissed her on the cheek and watched her reluctantly walk away before closing the front door.

Jogging up the stairs, I stripped out of my tank top and basketball shorts before getting in the shower.

"Babe, we gotta find someone new. Sadie's getting clingy." I wrapped my arms around Erica's waist.

"Damn already? I like her. She gives good head."

"Better than me?"

"Nobody is better than you." Erica turned around to face me.

"That better be your answer."

"Are you getting jealous, Luv?"

"Never that. I know my place here," I placed one hand on her heart, "and here." I slipped a finger inside of her, causing Erica to gasp.

"You play too much."

"Who's playing?" I pushed her to the back of the shower and up against the wall. She moaned as I rubbed my thumb over her clit while sliding two fingers in and out.

"Jooo, you're gonna make me cum, again."

"That's the point," I curved my finger and stroked her G-Spot, then started kissing and sucking on her neck. Erica mumbled incoherently and grabbed onto my shoulder for support, rocking her hips back and forth. I knew she was close, so I withdrew my fingers, dropped to my knees, and sucked hard on her clit. She only lasted about thirty more seconds before she was cursing out loud and calling my name. I slurped as she shivered and tapped me to stop.

"Baaabeee cut it out. I don't have any more
energy. That's like the third one tonight. I can't take
anymore."

After a few more tongue strokes, I complied
and stood up. Erica pulled me in for a kiss, licking the
taste of herself off my lips.

"Mmmm, I might have the energy for one
more," she mumbled in between kisses.

"Your wish is my command." I dropped back to
my knees before she could protest. This time I slid a
finger inside of her before sucking her clit into my
mouth.

"Oh damn!" She held onto the wall while I went
to work.

⊲◆⊳

I rolled over to an empty bed in the morning.
Erica walked out of the bathroom fully dressed.

"I thought you were going in late." I stretched and reached for her. She swatted at my hands and scurried out of my reach.

"It is late. It's almost 11."

"Oh damn. I never sleep this late."

"That's 'cause me and Sadie put it down on you last night."

I rolled my eyes and laid back down, "oh, okay."

"Speaking of Sadie, I want to give her another chance. I really like her." Erica sat on the edge of the bed.

"Whatever you say, baby, but you know the rules - if anyone starts getting attached, then it's a wrap. The last thing we want is someone coming between us."

"No one is ever coming between us. I promise. If you want her gone, then she's gone." She leaned over and kissed me softly on the lips.

"We'll talk about it later."

"Okay, but don't forget, I'm going out with Samantha after work. If it gets late, then I might just crash at her house."

"Ugh, why?"

"Because I don't drink and drive."

"I meant why are you going out with Sam?"

"Don't start, Jo. She's still your sister and my best friend. At some point, you are going to have to forgive her for your birthday. It's been six months now."

"I know how long it's been. I forgive her. I'm just not particularly fond of her right now."

"I understand, but please don't put me in the middle of that. I love you both."

"I'm not. We don't have to talk about this again. I know where you stand. Have a good day. I'll talk to you later."

"Okay, I love you." She looked more serious than she usually was.

"I love you more." I grabbed her and pulled her on top of me for a goodbye kiss.

"Dammit, Jo, you're going to wrinkle my dress."

She was fussing, but she was laughing at the same time. She finally broke free and jumped up. She popped me on the arm as she straightened her dress. When she got to my bedroom door, she looked back and blew me a kiss, and I pretended to catch it. We were so corny, but man, I was so happy.

2. SAMANTHA

"Why don't you two tell me what you have discussed since our last session?" Dr. Lacey crossed her legs and picked up her notepad.

"I don't know what more he wants from me. I apologized for everything with Rose, yet every conversation still turns into an argument about her." I was glad this was our last therapy session. Although I don't think it did us any good.

"I want Samantha to tell me why."

"And I told you I couldn't answer that because I really don't know. Besides, does it matter?"

"You making out with someone after agreeing to marry me doesn't matter? What the hell kind of reasoning is that?"

"Okay, let's pause for a second. Darrin, what do you think knowing "why" will accomplish for you?"

"I don't know exactly, but I just feel like in order to move forward, I need to know. I gave her everything and still-"

"This wasn't about you, Darrin. It wasn't even about Rose. This was about me finding myself and being true to myself. I didn't intend to hurt you in the process, and for that, I will never forgive myself."

"Darrin, what do you have to say to that? Can you accept that this wasn't about you?"

"I don't know. And the fact that she's barely let me touch her since that night and forget sex. We have not had sex since then either! Samantha may have agreed to come to counseling, but she didn't really give this relationship a try."

"Samantha, what do you have to say to those allegations, that you didn't give the relationship a try?"

"I did try, but I didn't think it was fair to pretend when it came to sex."

"Pretend? Really Samantha?"

"I'm sorry, and maybe pretend isn't the right word, but-"

"Samantha, have you made your decision about moving?" Dr. Lacey asked.

I sighed and looked down at my hand in my lap before answering.

"I have and I'm not going. I can't leave my family and-"

"And Rose?" Darrin asked dryly.

I chose to ignore that question, "Will you still take the transfer?"

"Yes. I turned it down before I proposed because I knew you would never leave your sisters. Then I asked for the transfer after because I figured if we worked out, it would be a fresh start for us, and if we didn't, it would be a fresh start for me. So, I guess it's off to Spain I go."

"How does that make you feel, Samantha?"

"Like, maybe that's the best thing for him. I hope you can find the happiness you deserve there."

"Yeah, me too."

<hr>

"Hey, Erica." I opened the door wide to let her enter.

"Why aren't you dressed yet?" She asked immediately after seeing me in leggings and a t-shirt.

"Not sure if I feel up to going out." I plopped down on my couch and grabbed a throw pillow.

"What's wrong?" Erica sat in the chair next to the couch.

"I feel horrible after my last counseling session with Darrin. Just between us, I only agreed to go to counseling so that I could say with a clear conscience that I tried my best, but I had pretty much already made up my mind about our relationship. With that being said, today was still harder than I thought it would be. Letting him know that I was not moving with him to Spain and that we were really done was hard. He cried, I cried. He's been mostly angry these last six months, so seeing his vulnerable side reminded me of why I fell in love with him in the 1st place."

"I'm sorry, boo. Are you having second thoughts about your decision?"

"No, not at all. I know I made the right decision for him and for me. I only wish I hadn't hurt so many people in the process, ya know?"

"Yeah, I understand that, and everyone is going through their healing process right now. In time, I'm sure everything will be back to normal. Have you talked to Rose?"

"Not really. Mainly through text."

"Are you two going to give it a real shot? What's she saying?"

"Not much, which is driving me crazy. She said she won't even entertain that conversation until I am 100% done with Darrin. I sent her a text earlier and asked if we could get together to talk this weekend. She said she'd let me know when she gets off her shift."

"So, she's playing hard to get?" Erica laughed.

"If that's what you want to call it. Whatever it is, I'm just trying to be as patient with her as she was with me. I owe us that much to see if there is a future. I'm scared that she's moved on. Her so-called-friend that she brought to my birthday party was really pretty, and she was all over Rose." I teared up at the thought that I had lost Rose before she was really mine.

"She was aight, but she ain't got nothing on my best friend! You know it's going to take more than a cute face to replace you. Besides, Rose told you they weren't dating. Don't trip, boo. Rose is just trying to protect herself. You guys will be okay." Erica smiled.

"I wish I had your confidence."

"You should have my confidence. Now, if we're not going out, then order some food, and I'll make some drinks after I get my bag out of the car. But I'm not gonna sit here and have a pity party with you, so decide what you want to do." Erica stood up and put her hands on her hips, waiting for my response.

"Okay fine, what you want to eat? I refuse to put real clothes on." I picked up my cell phone off the coffee table so that I could order food.

3. CHARLOTTE

"Hey, baby! How was your day?" I yelled out when I heard Michael coming in our garage door.

"Better now." He leaned over the couch to give me a kiss before walking into the kitchen. He came back with a bottle of water and sat down on the couch. "Did Danielle leave for Janelle's house already?"

"Yep, she left about 20 minutes ago. Since Janelle's mom picked her up, I told her we'd come get her on Sunday."

"Okay, cool. Does that mean you're not feeding me tonight since the kid is gone?"

I peeked out from the magazine I was flipping through. "You can have whatever you like as long as it does not involve me getting off this couch while you rub my feet."

"So let me get this straight. You were off today, but you want me to rub your feet after my long day of work?"

"What's wrong with that?" I wiggled my feet on his lap and smiled.

"Why you not rubbing my feet?" He started kicking his shoes off.

"Ain't nobody touching those things without gloves!" I laughed loud and hard.

"Oh, you got jokes!" He grabbed my feet and started tickling the bottoms.

I yelled "stop" and "cut it out" between laughs, all while trying unsuccessfully to get my feet back from his grip.

"Wait! Stop! This is Dr. Fuller calling." I was still laughing when I answered the phone. "Hey, Dr. Fuller." I sat up as the doctor started talking, and my jaw dropped in disbelief. "Are you sure?" Michael's face was instantly serious and concerned. "Okay… okay… yes… Monday at 9 o'clock… we'll see you then. Thank you." I hung up the phone and looked at my husband, who I'm pretty sure was holding his breath.

"What's wrong?"

"I'm, I'm pregnant," I said in shock.

"What? How? I thought they said-"

"I know, I know, but I'm about ten weeks. She wants us to come in Monday morning to run some more tests and discuss a plan." I could literally see Michael's brain working as he tried to gather his thoughts. "We were so blessed to finally have Dani, but you know I've always wanted more children. Michael, I'm scared. What if I miscarry again? I can't go through that again." I started crying. Michael immediately jumped into action. He slid closer to me and pulled me into his lap.

"Hey baby, let's not go there. We're going to wait until we talk to Dr. Fuller Monday and see what she says. Everything will be okay. God, please let everything be okay." He half-whispered the last sentence as he rocked me and wiped away my tears while kissing my forehead.

4. ROSE

"Detective Hathaway." I flashed my badge to the officer as I walked up the stairs entering the apartment that was my latest crime scene. "Hey, Max, what we got tonight?" I asked the investigator on the scene.

"A real bad domestic situation. The neighbor said she heard the couple arguing, things breaking, and our victim screaming, and then it was silent, so she called 9-1-1. When we got here, the suspect was gone, and our victim was unconscious in the bedroom. You just missed her leave in the ambulance about five minutes ago. She's beaten up pretty bad."

"Shit. You got any names?" I walked into the bedroom and looked around. It was clear they were fighting in here. Broken glass, a hole in the wall, even the tv was askew on the wall. I picked up a picture off the floor near the bed just as the investigator read off the names from his notepad.

"Yeah, our victim is Gloria Jackson, and the suspect is Brandy Warren."

I sat down on the bed, staring at the picture in my hand. It was my Gloria from college and Bran from the club.

"Hathaway, you okay? You look like you just saw a ghost. Hathaway? Detective?"

<hr>

"Hey. You still want to meet?"

"Hey, I wasn't expecting to meet tonight. It's late, Erica's here, and I've been drinking."

"Oh…okay."

"Rose, what's wrong?"

"Nothing, I just got off a long shift. I'll talk to you tomorrow."

"Why don't you come by here?"

"I'm good. We can talk tomorrow."

"I can tell that you're not good. If you don't come to me, then I'll just have to drive to you."

"Don't play like that, Sam. You just said you've been drinking."

"Then I'll see you when you get here. The door will be unlocked." And then she hung up.

I sat in my car debating if I should go, but I knew she was serious. If I didn't show up, she would come to me, and I didn't know what type of shape she was in to drive. I guess there really wasn't anything to debate.

When I got to Sam's place, I was half hoping that she had fallen asleep. I climbed the stairs and opened her bedroom door. She was sitting up in bed, surrounded by her tens of thousands of throw pillows, flipping through the channels.

"Hey," I said quietly, standing in the doorway.

"Hey yourself, come in and close the door. I don't want to wake up Erica. She's right down the hall."

I came in and sat on the edge of her bed, pushing the door to a little. Samantha got up and closed the bedroom door all the way. When she got closer, I grabbed her and put my head on her stomach. I wrapped my arms around her waist and just sat like that.

"Rose, what's going on? Are you okay?" I could hear the panic in her voice, but I couldn't talk, so I just squeezed her tighter. She finally put her arms on my shoulders and rubbed my head.

"Can I stay over?" I finally asked.

"Of course. Do you want to shower? I think I still have some of your clothes here." I nodded my head yes and let her go so that I could stand up.

"You know where the towels and washcloths are. I'll find you something to put on."

When I got out of the shower, a pair of sweats and a tank top were folded neatly on the sink. I got dressed and entered the bedroom to find Samantha sitting up in the bed again. I laid down next to her, put my head in her lap, and almost immediately fell asleep.

When I woke up the next morning, Sam wasn't in bed. Checking the clock on the nightstand, it was after nine, which was late for me. I grabbed my work cell to call my captain. I needed to let her know that I knew Gloria and Bran. I wasn't sure if I wanted to work the case or not, but it might not be my decision. It was up to my captain.

"Yes, Cap, I understand. Thank you."

I grabbed my clothes and headed downstairs to find Samantha. She was sitting on her patio with Erica drinking coffee. Last time I was on that patio-I wouldn't let myself finish the thought. Samantha's face lit up when she saw me coming towards the door.

"Hey, Erica." I bent over and hugged her.

"Heeeey Rose." She smiled questioningly, and Samantha made a face at her.

"Can I talk to you for a second?" I looked at Samantha.

She followed me to the living room.

"You're leaving?" She asked when she saw my things on the couch.

"Yes. I have to go into the precinct about a case."

"Are you going to tell me what was wrong last night?"

"I can't right now. Can we get together later?"

"Yeah, we can do that."

"Thank you. Can I have a hug?"

She smiled and nodded.

I held her a little tighter and longer than usual, and I knew she could sense that something was still bothering me. When I finally let go, I could read the concern in her eyes. I kissed her softly on the lips before grabbing my stuff and heading out.

5. ERICA

As soon as Samantha and Rose went into the house, I grabbed my phone and sent a text to Jo.

```
Erica: Babe, guess who stayed the night at
your sister's house?

Jo: You already told me you were staying
over there.

Erica: Not me, smart ass.

Jo: Okay, then who?

Erica: ROSE!

Jo: Word?

Erica: Yep! Did she say anything to
you? Sam said she called her upset
last night and ended up crashing over
here.  I think she's about to leave,
so I'll text you when I have more
info!

Jo: Nope. I haven't talked to her in
a few days. Aight, let me know.
```

Samantha strolled back outside to the patio.

"Everything okay?" I asked nonchalantly.

"Yeah, everything is good. You want to go get something to eat?"

"Uh uh. What's the tea? Y'all back together or what?"

"I told you what happened last night. We haven't talked about us at all. I'm just being a good friend."

"Girl bye. Good friend, my ass. The way you came back out here smiling and blushing. Something is definitely up."

"I promise I don't have any news other than we getting together later. Oh, and she kissed me!"

"For real?! Oh, it's a wrap then. You back in there sis. I told you, you didn't have anything to worry about!"

"I don't want to get my hopes up. I still don't know what's going on with her. She might want to talk about that. Either way, that kiss was nice. I damn sure missed that feeling." Samantha touched her lips and smiled.

"Aww best fran you missed your boo!" I laughed.

"Whatever! Let's go eat!"

"Okay, okay, damn, can I get dressed first?" We both got up from the table and went into the house to get dressed.

I decided to drive my own car so that I could run some errands after brunch. I was planning on going to the grocery store, but Jo texted me while we were eating, asking what I needed so she could get groceries for her place and mine. Since I didn't have to go to the grocery store, I decided to stop by the mall and pick up a few things. After grabbing a couple of new candles and some aromatherapy stuff from Bath and Body Works, I stopped by Victoria's Secret.

"Excuse me, can you help me find something?"

Sadie's eyes popped a little when she saw me, "yes ma'am. How can I help you?"

"Can you size me for a new bra?"

"Yes ma'am. Please follow me to the dressing room." I walked behind Sadie, watching her plump, round ass as we walked through the store. Once she closed the door behind us in the dressing room, I immediately went in.

"What's your issue, Sadie? I thought you understood the arrangement we had."

"I don't have an issue. I just asked if you guys would be calling me soon."

"No, you asked if Jo would be calling you soon. Don't get it twisted. Jo and I are one. All conversations are shared, and all rules are made together. So, anything you say to either of us, you say to both of us."

"I know. I wasn't trying to be disrespectful-"

"Oh, I know that, 'cause I know you not crazy." I cut her off. "Now, since you asking all these extra questions and acting thirsty, we have to find a new girl." Sadie's eyes got wide, but she didn't speak. "Let me make this clear, you are around because we BOTH want you to be, and if at any time we decide we don't want you, then you won't be. So, IF we decide to call you again, you need to remember your place. Do you understand?"

"Yes."

"Good. Now excuse me, I need to get back to my shopping." She stepped to the side, allowing me to squeeze by and exit the dressing room.

I sat in my car in the mall parking lot, aggravated. I made a decision that I hoped Jo would be okay with. I shot her a text and told her that I was cooking dinner tonight. She replied that she could be there by 7. Perfect, I had enough time to make dinner, shower, and get sexy before she got there. Ooh, that little lacy red teddy I bought last week will be perfect for tonight, I thought to myself as I backed out of my parking space.

6. SAMANTHA

I decided not to sit around my house looking stupid, waiting for Rose. After brunch, Erica asked me if I wanted to go to the mall with her, but I decided to go to the park instead. I had a blanket in my trunk and the Kindle app on my iPad. I found a shady spot under a tree and laid out my blanket before sitting down. I opened my Kindle app to the book I started reading last week, but no matter how hard I tried, I couldn't get into it. My mind kept wandering off to Rose. I was trying not to get too excited about her coming to me last night because, clearly, something was wrong. But just knowing that I was the person she ran to despite whatever she was going through gave me hope for us. Damn, I missed her so much—all the late-night talks and hanging out and making out. I smiled to myself. Just then, my phone dinged with a text notification.

Rose: Hey.

Sam: Hey, what's up?

Rose: Nothing much. You want to have dinner with me tonight?

Sam: Yeah, that sounds good. I was trying to keep it cool.

Rose: You want to eat out or stay in?

Hell, I wanted to stay in so she could eat me out, but that's probably not keeping it cool, I thought to myself.

Sam: Umm, let's order in.

Rose: Is 7 o'clock at my place okay with you?

Sam: Yeah, that's fine. See you later. I resisted adding a kissy face.

Rose: See you later.

So, I definitely won't be getting any reading done now. I stayed at the park for another 30 minutes, just listening to music and relaxing before I finally packed up my stuff to go. When I got home, I took a shower and laid across my bed to watch mindless TV.

I must have dozed off because I woke up and it was almost dark outside, and a glance at the clock on my nightstand said 7:45. I grabbed my phone, and there were several missed calls and text messages from Rose.

The last one said if I didn't call or text her in twenty minutes, then she was coming to find me. That was fifteen minutes ago. I quickly called her.

"Hello!"

"Hey. I'm sorry I fell asleep watching TV. Let me throw something on, and I'll be right over."

"Dammit Samantha! I thought maybe you got into an accident or something."

"Sorry. It wasn't intentional. Do you want me to pick up the food on the way?"

"No, I cooked."

"You cooked?"

"Yes, I cooked. I do know how to cook, and I wanted to do something special for you."

"Rose, I said I was sorry."

"It's okay. I had a long day. Just get here soon and safely please." She sounded more like herself.

"I'll be there in twenty minutes."

"Okay."

I hopped off my bed and ran into the bathroom. After brushing my teeth and washing my face, I pulled my hair up into a ponytail. I grabbed a jean jacket to throw on over my shirt and shorts and headed out the door. I pulled up in Rose's driveway with a minute to spare. I took that minute to take a few deep breaths and try to push away the memory of my last night here, my first and last night with Rose. I closed my eyes, thinking how perfect it was. I could still feel every curve of her body, and in my mind, I could still taste her. Lost in my memories, I opened my eyes, and she was standing on her porch, her hands in her pockets, watching me. I got out of the car and smiled as I walked towards the door.

"Hey." She smiled at me.

"Hey yourself."

When I got to the top of the stairs, she pulled me in for a tight hug.

"Damn, I missed you," she said into my neck.

"You just saw me this morning." I joked back despite being in heaven in her arms.

"I see you're still as sarcastic as ever. Come in." She let me go but grabbed my hand to lead me into the house.

After a delicious dinner of cajun shrimp pasta and breadsticks, we retired to the couch. Rose handed me my favorite blanket and a glass of wine. She sat on the opposite end of the couch as me. After a few minutes of quiet, I finally broke the silence.

"Can you tell me what last night was about now?"

"Actually, I can't. It was about a case at work, so I can't really talk about it. I hope you understand."

"Of course, I understand. It must be a bad one. I've never seen you like that before."

"It is, but I'll be okay. I would rather talk about us."

"Okay. You first."

"Haha, no. I think you should go first." She leaned back and folded her arms.

Great, I thought to myself. Here goes nothing or everything.

7. JOSEPHINE

"Honey, I'm home!" I yelled as I walked in the front door of Erica's apartment.

"Very funny. I'll be down in a second. Have a seat!" She yelled back from upstairs.

I walked through the kitchen on my way to the living room, stopping by the stove to see what smelled so good. Just as I was about to lift a lid off of one of the pots, Erica yelled, "get out of my kitchen!"

"Damn, I'm just getting a drink!"

"Whatever, get you a beer and go sit down!"

I rolled my eyes and grabbed a beer out of the fridge before sitting on the couch. I started looking for the remote to turn the tv on when suddenly Erica's voice was closer, "I have something else you can turn on."

I looked up to see her standing in the doorway wearing a red, lacy, strappy number and matching stiletto high heels.

"Damn, girl." My mouth dropped, and I'm pretty sure I drooled a little bit.

"You ready to eat?"

"Ab-so-damn-lutely." I jumped up from the couch and headed towards her.

"Dinner, Jo. Are you ready for dinner?" She put her hands on my chest to create space between us.

"Fuck dinner. I'm not hungry. I'm horny."

"Jo."

"Dammit, E, then why did you come down here dressed like that?" I groaned and walked back to the couch. "Can I get something stronger to drink than a beer? Especially if you're about to make me sit through dinner while you're half-naked."

"You are so dramatic. I'll get you a shot. This is a practice in discipline and delayed gratification. You said you are always down to try something new."

"I wasn't aware at the time I made that statement that it would involve torture."

Erica handed me a double shot of Crown Peach. I gave her the evil eye through slanted eyes and threw the shot back. She bent over and licked my lips softly, tasting the liquor, then she nibbled my ear and whispered, "if you really want torture, we can try that next week." When she stood up, the look she gave me, I thought she might actually be serious. She took the shot glass from me and turned around to walk into the kitchen. Her high, round ass was accentuated with red straps on her hips that connected to a thong, or at least I assumed a thong because I couldn't see anything but her cheeks. This woman and her body were going to be the death of me.

"I'm going to the bathroom."

"Okay, baby. I'm going to make your plate. Oh, and Jo?"

"Yeah?" I stopped at the door to the half bathroom off the hallway.

She peeked around the corner with a smirk, "the feminine wipes are under the sink. In case you need to take care of that situation you got going on." She twirled her finger towards my groin area.

I didn't even know what to say, so I just slammed the bathroom door.

About halfway through my meal of steak, mashed potatoes, and asparagus, Erica casually stated, "I went to see Sadie today."

"Really? Why?"

"I don't know. It wasn't really planned. I went to the mall, and it just kind of happened."

"So, you went to the mall 30 minutes away just because? I thought we agreed we would talk more about the decision later?"

"I just wanted to…clear the air."

"So now that the air is clear?"

Erica sighed and looked away nervously. Which was entirely out of character for her, so I got kind of nervous.

"Well, I was thinking," she started and stopped.

I was trying my best to be patient, but what the hell was she going to say that had her so nervous? Did she want to see other people? I knew this threesome shit was a bad idea.

"I was thinking we would cool it on the threesomes for a while. There are other ways we can keep our sex life interesting. Not that we really need any help in that department."

I was so relieved that I burst out laughing. Erica did not find anything funny. She got up from the table, picked up our plates, and went into the kitchen. I took a moment to compose myself before following her.

"Baby," I approached her with caution. The last thing I wanted was to fight, especially with her dressed like that. I was already horny, and even though an argument would turn me on, I knew Erica was the exact opposite; even if we made up after, she would still be mad and not give me none.

"Can we finish the conversation?"

"Don't worry about it, Jo. I'm not particularly in the mood to be laughed at."

"Erica, I wasn't laughing at you. I want to talk about it."

I grabbed her hand and turned her around to face me. "I promise I was not laughing at you. I was so nervous thinking about what you were going to say that I started laughing with relief. You know I care about everything you have to say. Please come sit down and talk." I pulled her, full pouting lips and all, to the living room. We sat down on the couch facing each other, and I held on to her hands.

"What makes you want to stop the threesomes? I thought you were enjoying them."

"I was, but the whole thing with Sadie didn't sit right with me. I know we completely trust each other, or else we wouldn't be comfortable bringing in another person. However, just the thought that she was bold enough to come at you just made me think how naive we are for thinking that the next person wouldn't attempt to disrespect what we have. I just don't want to take that chance. It's not worth it, to me anyway." She looked away from me with her last statement.

I let go of her hand and gently turned her face back to me, "Okay."

"Okay?"

"Okay. We decided to do this together with the understanding that if at any time either of us wanted to stop, we would. I don't need anybody but you. That was fun but definitely not necessary to keep me satisfied or happy. Just you baby and more of these outfits."

"Are you sure?"

"Listen, just like we made that decision together, we can decide today that if at any point we are not happy, sexually or otherwise, we talk about it. We try to fix whatever it is together. I promise you I will do that."

"I promise too."

"Now I promise I'm about to make your ass pay for making me sit here for the last hour while you damn near naked."

"Ooh, I'm gonna hold you to that promise." She straddled my lap and pulled my shirt off before kissing me deeply.

"Bro, you home? I need to stop by real quick. Cool, I'll be there in about 10 minutes." I grabbed my duffel bag and locked up the club. Pulling my fitted cap down to hide my face as I made my way to my car in the parking lot.

"What's up?" Tre answered the door, letting me into her apartment.

"I gotta go out of town for a couple days, and I need a favor."

"Okay. What you need?"

"Some cash. I need to get a new bank card, but I can't wait until the bank opens to leave."

"Sure. How much?"

I followed Tre towards her office. "A couple thousand."

Tre stopped in the middle of the hallway, "A couple - I don't keep that kind of cash in the house. Why can't you go to the bank on Monday when you get to where you're going? Where are you going?"

"Umm I don't know yet, and you know Monday is a holiday, plus I just don't want to have to stop."

"Bran, what's going on? You acting even more weird than usual."

"Man, you not gonna believe me anyway."

"What's new? I usually don't believe all your crazy stories, but it's never stopped you from telling them anyway." She started to laugh but stopped when she realized how serious I was.

"You know the chick I been seeing off and on for the last couple months or so? Gloria?" Tre nodded yes that she remembered. "Me and her got into a heated argument about one of my other females. Anyway, one thing led to another, and I hit her."

"Dammit Bran!"

"But I swear I only slapped her. Then she went crazy. She hit me back and started screaming, throwing herself into the wall, hitting herself, breaking shit. Just fucking crazy! She ran head first into the wall, and next thing I knew, she was unconscious!"

"Whoa, what?! Did you call an ambulance? Is she okay?!"

"I don't know. I panicked, and I ran! I've been staying at one of the clubs in case the cops are looking for me, but I think I need to get out of town."

"Or turn yourself in! Do you even know if she made it to the hospital? What the hell is wrong with you? Do you really expect me to believe that she beat herself up and you had nothing to do with it?"

"I know you don't believe me, but it's the truth. Man, I swear! I need help!"

"Well, I'm not helping you run away from no shit like this. Did you call Jo?"

"Hell no. You already know what Jo's reaction is gonna be. I just need to lay low for a couple days until I find out that Gloria is okay, and she can tell everyone what really happened. She'll clear my name. I know she will."

"You can crash here so I can keep an eye on you, and if she doesn't 'clear your name' in 24 hours, you will turn yourself in. Give me your car keys."

"Damn, it's like that? You don't trust me?"

"Hell no, I don't trust you. You just told me your girlfriend beat herself up to the point of unconsciousness. I don't know if she should be committed or you. If it weren't for the fact that we've been friends since kindergarten, I would be calling the cops right now. So, give me your fucking keys before I change my damn mind and do just that."

"Alright, bro, chill. Here, damn."

I tossed her my car keys and walked past her into the living room since it was clear I wasn't going anywhere. I should have known coming here would be

a mistake. For all that, I might as well have called Jo's
righteous ass.   57

9. ROSE

"Good morning, Captain." I eased off the couch, trying my best not to wake up Samantha. I went to my room so I could talk privately. "Yes, ma'am. I will turn over the report and all my contacts to Detective Moore right away. Yes ma'am. You're welcome." I sat on the edge of my bed after hanging up the phone. I still had so many mixed emotions with this whole situation that I had yet to process. I was surprised that Gloria was with a woman after how she treated me and actually a little angry. Not to mention mad as hell that Bran had beat her up. No matter my feelings for Gloria, I didn't wish any harm to her. I know turning the case over was the right thing to do, but part of me still wanted to be the investigator. Luckily, Detective Moore and I were cool, so I might be able to find out what was going on with the case. My next big decision was if I told Samantha. We were trying to start fresh, and I didn't want to start with an omission of the truth.

"You okay, babe?" I was so deep in thought that I hadn't heard Sam come up the stairs. She was standing in the doorway to my bedroom wearing one of my oversized t-shirts.

"Yeah, I'm good. I had a work call, and I didn't want to wake you."

"Is it about the same case from the other night?" She sat on the bed and crossed her legs.

"Uhhh yeah. I've been reassigned, so I have to turn over my stuff to the new investigator."

"Oh wow. Are you okay with the case being reassigned?"

"Kind of. It was for the best."

"It must have been really bad. I'm glad you won't be..."

"It's Gloria." I blurted out.

"Huh? What's Gloria?"

"The case. Gloria was beaten up pretty bad by someone she was dating." I purposely did not mention Bran. I couldn't disclose that information and risk Bran being tipped off.

"Is she okay?"

"She's in a medically induced coma to allow the swelling on her brain to go down."

"Oh my God! She was beat that bad? What kind of man would do that?"

"There are all types of monsters in this world, baby." I reached across the bed and grabbed her hand. She scooted closer to me and rested her head on my shoulder.

"How are you after seeing her in that state? After seeing her at all? I mean, it's been a while, right?"

"It's been over ten years. I actually haven't seen her, just a picture. She was already transported to the hospital by the time I arrived on the scene. I thought about going to the hospital to see her but I...I just couldn't."

"Are you still in love with her?"

"No," I answered without any hesitation. "I don't think I ever really was. I loved her, yes, but now knowing what it feels like to be in love, that wasn't it back then. This is it now."

"How can you be so sure?"

"About which part?"

"Both parts. Not being in love with her? Being in love with me?"

"Well, for one, I've matured enough to be able to tell the difference. The feeling isn't the same, the connection isn't the same, and I'm not the same. How about you?"

"If you're asking if I'm in love with you, then the answer is yes. I'd like to think I'm a different person than I was when we met over a year ago, that this experience has changed me, but honestly, I'm still a little scared about us. Don't get me wrong. I know that I want to be with you. I'm just nervous."

"That's understandable as it is with any new relationship but particularly one this, different. But Samantha, I need to know you're really in this with me. We can go as slow as you need to. Matter 'fact, I would prefer if we did go slow and really date each other. If you're having second thoughts or need more time, then tell me. I will not knowingly put myself in other situationships. I just can't do that shit anymore. I know what I bring to the table, and I'm prepared to eat alone if necessary."

"Damn, listen, I know I put you through a lot, and I'm sorry. I will prove to you that I'm serious about us and that I'm not just here to have my cake and eat it too. I'm committed to seeing where this relationship goes. I promise."

"I believe you." I couldn't help but think, so did Darrin. "So, Ryan and his wife are having a barbecue later, and I want you to come with me. Do you have anything planned?"

"Not really. Do they know about…me?"

"Ummm, Sam, I've been out for about fifteen years now, and Ryan and I have been friends just as long. So, there's nothing to worry about there."

"I meant, do they know about what happened between us? Our history?"

"Oh, Ryan does, but not Sara. Then again, he probably told her. Either way, don't worry about it. They'll be cool. They also know how important you are to me."

"Rose, I don't know."

"How about this? We go, and if you feel uncomfortable in any way, then I promise we will leave immediately. Deal?"

"Okay, that's fair."

"Cool, I'll pick you up at six." I stood up from the bed, pulling her up with me.

"Why do I feel like you're putting me out?" Samantha laughed.

"Because I am. I have to go into the station for a little bit, so I need to get ready to head over there." I pulled her in for a hug to soften the fact that I was very much serious about her leaving.

"Ohhhkaaaay, I guess." She said with a slight pout after I let her go.

"Lemme walk you out."

"Nah, I'm good. I know the way." She sounded a little salty.

"Babe, don't be mad."

"I'm fine. I'll see you later." She kissed me on the cheek and walked out of my bedroom.

A few minutes later, I heard the front door close. I sat down on my bed. As much as I loved Sam and wanted to be with her, there was still a part of me that didn't fully trust her, and I questioned if I could be in a relationship with someone I didn't trust. I picked up my phone to text Ryan. I hadn't told him that me and Sam were 'dating', so I wanted to give him a heads up that I was bringing her to the barbecue. Before I could even scroll to his name, my work phone rang.

"Hathaway."

"Detective Hathaway, I'm calling to inform you that Gloria Jackson is awake and is asking for you."

"Oh, thank you for letting me know. I will let the new investigator know that she is awake. Is she able to answer questions?"

"She can answer questions. And detective, she asked for you specifically by name."

"She did? Okay, I'll be there in a couple hours."

Great.

Tre: Hey, we got a situation with Bran. Can't get into it via text, but I need you to stop by my place in the morning.

Jo: Aight. What the hell she do now?

Tre: Man, I'll see you in the morning. Text me when you're on the way and when you get here.

Bran was going to be pissed that I involved Jo, but I really didn't know what else to do. Could I believe the crazy-ass story she told me or trust that she would do what she was supposed to do? I checked my security cameras to see if she was still sleeping on the couch and turned on the alarm system before getting in the bed. I can't believe Bran had us in this shit again.

I awoke to a text from Jo saying she would be there in ten minutes. Shit, I forgot she was on military time. It was only 5:30. I rechecked the security cameras before going into the bathroom. Bran was still knocked out. By the time I brushed my teeth, washed my face, and pulled my locs back into a ponytail, Jo was texting that she was at the door.

I went outside to fill her in before we went to confront Bran together.

"Are you fucking kidding me?!" Jo all but yelled when I filled her in on Brandy's latest story and indiscretion. I just nodded my head because I knew Jo wasn't done. "I knew helping her get out of that situation when we were younger was gonna come back to bite us in the ass. I'm not putting my life or my pockets on the line for her ass again. THIS time she's getting some help, or I'm done!"

"I agree. We're on the same page. Now let's get her there. I know I'm the one that convinced you to help last time, and I know how hard that was for you. I just want you to know you aren't the only one that has lost sleep over it, and I'm sorry."

"Don't mention it. We're family, and that's what family does. We help each other, but we can't enable her anymore. I'm serious, Tre."

"I know, I know. Let's go talk to her." We walked back inside and down the hallway to the living room, only to find Bran was gone. Her backpack wasn't on the floor, and after a quick sweep, discovered she must have slipped out the back door.

"Shit. There's no telling where she's going or what she's going to do." Maybe calling Jo was a mistake. Bran had agreed she would turn herself in, but now.

"Don't worry about it. I'll handle it. I always do."

"What are you going to do?" I yelled. She was already out the door.

11. ERICA

This chick clearly wants me to curse her out again. I told her we would call if we were interested, but she has called me twice in the last hour. I hate to have to put hands on her.

    Sadie: Erica, please answer. I know
    you told me not to call, but I don't
    have anyone else to turn to. Please.

Hmmm, what could she have going on so urgent that she calls me for help? Before I could decide on answering, my phone dinged with another text notification.

    Jo: Hey Luv. I need to reschedule our plans
    for tonight. I have an emergency that I
    need to deal with. I'll call you as soon as
    I can. Love you.

    Erica: Hey baby. Okay, be careful. Love you
    back.

Well, damn idle hands and all.

    Erica: What Sadie?

Sadie: Thank you for texting back. I was scared you wouldn't. Can we meet?

Erica: Meet for what? I only answered because I'm bored, and it seemed important. What do you want?

Sadie: It is important. I told my mom about you.

Erica: You did what? Why the hell would you do that?

Sadie: I don't mean you specifically. I mean, I told her I like girls. I wasn't expecting her to answer the way she did. I don't know what to do, and I don't really have anybody else to turn to. Please, Erica.

Erica: Okay fine. I'll meet you at the Starbucks in Five Points in 30 minutes. This better not be bullshit, Sadie.

Erica: I promise it's not.   Thank you!

I walked into Starbucks twenty minutes later and spotted Sadie at a table in the corner. After ordering a passion fruit iced tea, I went to join her.

"Okay, I'm here. What's up?" I announced as I sat down at the table across her. She looked up with red, puffy eyes and tear-stained cheeks.

"Thanks for coming." She smiled a little.

"Sadie, what happened? I didn't know you weren't out to your mother."

"I just figured it was time to be true to myself and stop hiding, so I told her. And she said no daughter of hers would be a dyke, so if that's who I choose to be, then I'm dead to her. She wouldn't even let me say goodbye to my little sister. She said she doesn't want my gay spirit jumping into the only child she has." By this time, Sadie was bawling her eyes out, "I don't have any other family. They're all I have, Erica."

I reached my hand across the table and grabbed hers, "I'm so sorry, Sadie. I wish I knew the magic words to make you feel better, but I don't. I'm sorry." I honestly didn't know what to say, I could see the pain in her eyes, but I was at a loss for words. She was crying so hard that I finally slid into the seat next to her so she could put her head on my shoulder. I wrapped my arms around her and just let her cry. After what seemed like an eternity, the crying subsided a little. She sat up and grabbed a tissue from the box that one of the baristas had placed on the table.

"Did you drive here? Do you want me to drop you off at home or a friend's?" I asked quietly.

"I don't really have any friends here. I'm sorry for calling you. I know you told me to stay away. I just didn't know who else to turn to. I admire your strength and confidence so much. Thanks for coming but I'll be okay. I promise not to call anymore." She wiped her eyes, grabbed her bag, and went to the bathroom before I could say anything.

Don't do it, Erica. She's not your responsibility. She's not Cheri. Although those were the thoughts in my head, my heart was not listening. Something in me was saying, don't let her leave here alone. I know she wasn't Cheri, but maybe I could save her. I already knew what I was going to do; I was just trying to justify it in my head when I talked to Jo.

I sent her a text to call me "ASAP".

When Sadie came out of the bathroom, I stood up and grabbed her hand. I smiled and told her, "you are not alone, and they are not all you have. Okay?" Her eyes welled with tears, and she nodded her head yes.

⸺◁◆▷⸺

"Jo, what are you doing here?" I switched on the light on my nightstand to find her sitting on the foot of the bed. It was almost 1 o'clock in the morning.

"I missed you. I got your text and your voicemail, and I thought something might be wrong."

"Jo, that was hours ago! Why didn't you call me back?"

"I told you I was dealing with an emergency, and then I dropped my phone somewhere on the highway while riding. So, I figured I'd better just come since I couldn't call."

"What's wrong? Have you been drinking?"

"I had a couple of beers a little while ago, but I'm not drunk if that's what you're implying. You know I wouldn't be riding or driving if I was intoxicated."

"I know. Are you coming to bed?" I pulled the covers back and slid over so she could get in the bed.

"Not right now. I can't sleep. What did you want to talk about? Your voicemail seemed urgent." She kicked her boots off before getting up to stretch.

"We can talk about it tomorrow, baby. Why don't you tell me what's going on with you? Something has you upset." She didn't answer, just paced back and forth across my bedroom.

"Do you think I'm a horrible person?" She stopped pacing for a second and looked at me.

"What, of course, I don't. You're an amazing person Jo-"

"I do horrible things, though." She cut me off and started back pacing. "Did you know that the day my parents died, me and my dad got into a huge argument? I accused him of not accepting me for being gay and for judging me. He always accepted me, though. I was just angry because he didn't want me to join the military right out of high school. He wanted me to go to college first. So, I said horrible things to him-"

"Jo, I'm so-" I tried to interject, but at this point, I think she was talking more to herself than she was to me.

"A couple of hours later, the police were at our door telling us about the accident. I was so angry! Angry with him, angry with myself. I put Charlie through hell because I was so angry. I never told her what the argument was about. I promised myself that I wouldn't get that angry anymore, that I wouldn't stay angry at someone I loved like that. Yet here I am, being stubborn and stupid towards my damn twin sister! And for what? I feel like I'm letting everyone down. Am I letting you down?"

"Jo, baby, you're not-" Seeing her like this had me choked up. I was trying not to cry.

"I can't fix everything, though. I try to fix everything, you know. Cause I'm good at it. I can hold it together when most people fold, but I'm tired. I'm so tired, and I don't know if I can fix this. Not this time. I shouldn't have fixed it last time; I shouldn't have fixed it." Now she was crying and still pacing. I had never seen her cry before. I hopped out of bed and grabbed her.

"It's okay, baby. You don't have to fix anything. I'm here." She squeezed me tight and cried on my shoulder.

What in the hell was she talking about? What did she fix?

12. SAMANTHA

Why was I so worried about finally meeting Ryan and his wife? I've only heard good things about them. Maybe because I know they have heard more than good things about me. I don't think I'm ready to face other people that know about my past indiscretions. Maybe I should just tell Rose I'm not going. Ugh, but she's really looking forward to me coming, so I guess I need to suck it up and get dressed. I had been lying across my bed in a towel having this conversation with myself for at least 30 minutes, and since it was almost 6 o'clock, there was no backing out at this point anyway. I stretched as I walked into my closet just as my phone dinged with a text notification. A few minutes later, I emerged fully dressed in cut-off jean shorts, a strappy, midriff baring shirt, and wedges. I sat on the edge of the bed to put on my jewelry and check my phone.

Rose: Hey baby. I know you had reservations about going tonight, and I don't want you

Oh, hell no, not after I got myself psyched up and dressed to go. I shot her a text back.

I smiled and rolled my eyes at my phone, grabbed my purse, and jogged down the stairs. I opened the door to Rose, looking even better than usual. She was wearing a navy t-shirt with khaki joggers and a fresh pair of navy and white Jordan's. Her long hair was pulled back in her usual ponytail. I don't know if it was the six-month drought I was currently experiencing or what, but I swear my panties were instantly wet when she smiled at me.

"Hey beautiful." She gave me a big hug.

"Hey sexy," I said into her neck. "How was your day?"

"It was a day. You ready? By the way, these things usually run pretty late, so if you want to grab a bag, you can crash at my house."

"Nope. You won't be kicking me out again tomorrow morning. You can either drop me off home or crash here." I stated very matter-of-factly.

"Ohhhhkay then. I'm sure I have my gym bag in the car if needed."

"Great, let's go!"

Twenty minutes later, we pulled up in front of the prettiest house on the block. The lawn was perfectly manicured, there were rose bushes and even a white picket fence. Rose must have sensed my appreciation of the view.

"Ryan and Sara are quite the American dream family, picket fence included," she laughed.

"I see. I also see it's only a few cars here. Are we early?"

"Nah, this is the usual crowd—just a small gathering of family and friends. Don't be nervous. Everyone will love you."

"Thanks, babe. I'm okay. Can I ask a question before we go in?"

"Sure. What's up?"

"Are we a couple?" I turned in my seat to face her.

"Ummm, more like a couple of people dating. Wait, let me finish. I know we talked the other night, and you made your intentions very clear. But Samantha, I told you I wanted to go slow given the fact that you literally just got out of a long-term relationship a couple of days ago. What I would like is for us to exclusively date each other and continue to get to know one another. I know that I'm in love with you, but I don't want to rush into a committed relationship, not yet. Are you okay with that?"

I paused for a second before answering, "Honestly? I don't know, but I'm going to have to be if that's what it takes to be with you. I know what I put you through, so I'm willing to do whatever it takes to prove I'm really in this for the long haul."

Rose smiled and leaned over the armrest. She kissed me softly on the lips, "I do love you Samantha."

"I know and I love you too," I smiled back despite really feeling some type of way about the conversation. I mean, on the one hand, I understand what Rose is saying, but on the other hand, I feel like I'm being punished for what happened with Darrin. I guess it is what it is at this point. Rose opened my car door and grabbed my hand to help me out. She held my hand in hers as she closed the car door, and we walked up the walkway to the house.

A young, Hispanic-looking woman opened the door almost immediately after Rose rang the bell.

"Perfect timing, sis!" The woman hugged Rose, and I briefly saw a look of confusion on her face when she turned to greet me.

"You must be Samantha!" She pulled me in for a hug. She must have noticed my confused look as well. "You look like Josephine," she explained, laughing.

"Yes sis, this is my Samantha. Sam, this is Sara, Ryan's wife."

"So nice to finally meet you. I've heard so much about you."

"Likewise. Rose, now that you're here, maybe you can settle the dispute between Ryan and me about who asked who out first." Sara turned away from the door and walked down a hall. Rose smiled at me and grabbed my hand as we walked into the house. We followed Sara down the hall into a huge open kitchen and family room. About eight or nine people were sitting on barstools and couches throughout the area.

"Everybody, this is Samantha! Samantha, This is…" Rose went around the room, introducing me to everyone. "Where's Ryan?"

"He's outside finishing up the grill." Sara answered.

Rose motioned for me to follow her outside.

"What's good, bro?!" Rose yelled when we stepped out onto the deck. A tall, muscular, darker-skinned man with curly hair looked up from the grill and smiled. He also looked a little confused when he saw me, but he recovered quickly.

"It's about time you showed up!" He came from behind the grill and hugged Rose.

"Yeah, yeah, yeah. Bro, this is Samantha. Baby, this is Ryan."

Ryan gave me a big bear hug, lifting me off the ground.

"It's so good to finally meet you," Ryan said after he put me down.

"You, too." I laughed.

We stood around talking for a few minutes, and I felt completely at ease about being accepted.

"Samantha, do you mind going to tell everyone to come outside to eat?" Ryan asked.

"Of course not. I need to use the bathroom anyway."

"It's down the hallway off the kitchen, babe."

I nodded as I slid the patio door leading back into the kitchen.

"Hey everyone, Ryan said to come outside and eat."

There were murmurs of "finally" and "I'm starving" as the small group got up and headed outside. I didn't see Sara with the group, but I was too busy dancing to the bathroom to really notice. A few minutes later, while in the bathroom, I heard what sounded like Sara on the phone.

"Hey girl! Soooo change of plans. I'll explain later, but it looks like she's not single, so don't come over tonight! I'll call you tomorrow."

I washed my hands and exited the bathroom running into a startled Sara in the hallway.

"Hey Samantha, I didn't know anyone was in here. Did you eat?"

"No, not yet. I had to use the bathroom. Going to fix a plate now. Are you coming out to join us?"

"Yes! Let's go before those heathens eat it all." She linked her arm through mine, and we walked through the house and out onto the deck.

Shortly after we had all eaten, somebody broke out the cards, and I was drafted into being Sara's partner in Spades. Just as we sat down to play, Rose got a call on her work cell and stepped into the house to take it. Someone else was waiting to play, so we decided to play without her. I was so pumped that we won two - 500 point games back to back, that I didn't notice Rose wasn't back yet. I gracefully bowed out of a third-round and went to find her.

She was in the kitchen talking to some chick. Rose was leaning with her back against the counter drinking a mixed drink, and the girl was sitting on a chair at the island.

"Hey, everything okay?" I asked Rose.

"Yeah, I had a work call, and then I was talking to Denise. Denise, this is Samantha."

"Hi Samantha. I was just trying to convince Detective Rose to take me to the gun range so she can teach me how to shoot."

"Really? That sounds fun. When are you guys doing that?" I asked Rose, looking her dead in the eye.

"And I was just telling Denise that the way my schedule is set up, I don't think I would have time for something like that." Rose stared back.

"Your schedule, huh?" I questioned, cocking my head to the side.

"That's what I said! Her schedule can't be that busy where she can't fit in some fun!" Denise jumped in and put her hand on Rose's arm.

"Exactly, is your schedule really that busy, Detective Rose?" I gritted my teeth as Denise had not removed her hand off of Rose's arm yet.

Before Rose could respond, Sara walked into the kitchen behind me.

"Denise! You didn't get my message?"

"No. What's up?"

"Uhh, nevermind. Why don't you come get a plate and say hey to the rest of the gang?"

Denise slid off the stool, and I could see the crop top and skin-tight jeans she was wearing.

"See you outside, Detective." She said in a sultry voice before walking onto the deck. Sara looked embarrassed, and it dawned on me that it had been Denise that she left that message to tell her that

Rose wasn't single. She must have been trying to set them up.

As soon as the sliding door was closed, "so is she the reason you tried to convince me not to come?" I demanded.

"Considering I just met her 30 minutes ago, that doesn't seem plausible."

"Well, what the hell was that, Rose? I thought you said we were exclusive. Did you bring me over here to get even in front of your family and friends?" I felt myself getting upset and a little loud.

"Samantha, lower your voice, please." Rose was still leaned against the counter and still very much calm, which pissed me off even more.

"Don't tell me to lower my voice. In fact, take me home. Better yet, I'll find my own way home." I was steaming mad, and as I went to walk past her, she grabbed me and pinned me in place between her body and the counter.

"Rose let me-"

"What kind of person do you think I am? That's a rhetorical question, so I don't really need an answer right now. Do you really think that I would wait for you just to purposely embarrass you? I don't know that girl, nor do I care to know her. She's nowhere near my type, and you walked in as I was trying to let her down gently. I would have properly introduced you, but we don't exactly have a title at the moment. Now I'm not going to argue with you, especially not here, so let me say goodbye to my brother, and I will take you home. Okay?"

I had my arms folded against my chest, and I was trying not to let an angry tear escape, so I nodded.

"Samantha, this isn't going to work if we don't trust each other. And I need you to trust that I would never intentionally hurt nor disrespect you." She rubbed her thumb over my arm in an attempt to soften me up a little. It kind of worked.

"I trust you, and I know you wouldn't do anything to hurt me. I just got jealous; she was asking you out right in front of me, not to mention she had her hands on you."

"I was trying not to hurt her feelings, but I didn't intend to hurt yours. You know that, right?"

"Maybe." I responded a little playfully.

"Maybe? So, you gonna make me work for your forgiveness?"

I nodded, right before she nibbled my bottom lip. Her nibble turned into a soft kiss which turned into a deeper kiss. I unfolded my arms and pulled her in to deepen the kiss more. "Can we go?" I asked.

"Sounds like a good idea. Let's go say bye."

She kissed me again before shifting her body weight and letting me go. Before we walked outside, she grabbed and held my hand. It looked as if several people had already left, so only a few people were sitting around in the yard. Unfortunately, Denise was still there. Although she seemed to have cooled down a lot, she smiled and waved goodbye from across the yard. I guess Sara had told her what was up. I smiled and waved back. We hugged Sara and Ryan and made plans to get together soon.

When we got to my front door, Rose kissed me on the cheek and said, good night.

"You're not coming in?" I asked, confused and horny.

"I don't think that's a good idea."

"Why not?"

"I don't want to confuse things with sex. I feel like we did that last time."

"What's there to confuse? We both know what we want this time around. And I want to make love."

"I want that too, but I'm just not ready yet. I hope you understand."

She really is going to make ME work for this, "I understand, and I will be patient. After all, you did wait for me. Just because we aren't doing anything doesn't mean you can't stay over, though. We've stayed the night together plenty of times. I can behave." I wiggled my eyebrows at her like she did the first night we went out.

She laughed, "okay, I'll stay."

She went back to her car to grab her gym bag so she could change. Once in my bedroom, she stripped down to her boxer briefs and a tank top. By the time I got out of the bathroom from washing my face and wrapping my hair, she was in my bed sound asleep. I climbed in next to her and dozed off, smiling. This might not have been how I pictured the night ending, but at least she was here.

13. JOSEPHINE

I rolled over to an empty bed, again. This was becoming a habit that I did not like, I thought to myself as I sat up and looked around for Erica. I slid out of bed and went into the bathroom. There was a sticky note on the mirror: *Good morning, my love. I just ran out to get you a smoothie. I'll be right back.*

I smiled at the note and then frowned at my reflection in the mirror. My eyes were red and puffy from crying. I was mad at myself for having a breakdown, especially in front of Erica. I knew she would have a bunch of questions that I wasn't sure if I was ready to answer. So, I made a straight-up bitch move. I scribbled a note back to her about going to get a new phone and threw my clothes on. I was out the door and speeding off on my motorcycle within minutes.

I stopped by T-Mobile and grabbed a new phone on the way home. I plugged the phone up to charge while I showered and got dressed. When I checked the phone, there were two missed calls and a voicemail from Erica.

Josephine Nicole Riley, I don't know what you have going on right now, and I am trying to be patient, but so help me if you ever ghost me like that again. Just call me back. I love you.

Damn, she used my entire government name. I had to fix that and fast, but there were so many other things to fix. Where do I even start?

I sent her a text.

```
Jo: I'm sorry, baby. I didn't mean to ghost
you. I  have  some  things  to  handle.  I
promise I'll explain everything soon.   I
love you more.
```

Hopefully, that was enough to get me at least partially out of the doghouse. Then I sent a text to Charlie. That was a relationship that I've been seriously neglecting.

```
Jo: Hey, my beautiful big sister.  I just
wanted you to know I miss you, and I'm
sorry that I don't reach out as often as I
should.  I was thinking about me and Erica
```

This next conversation needs to be in person.

"Hello?"

"Hey Sam."

"Hi Jo."

"Can I come over? Or can we meet somewhere?"

Silence.

"Sam, please. I just want to talk."

"You can come over."

"Okay. I can be there in 15 minutes. Want me to bring you coffee or anything?"

"That's fine, and no, thank you."

She hung up before I could say anything else.

I drove my truck instead of the bike and stopped by Starbucks to pick up a Caramel Frappe for Sam. Even though she said no, I knew she could never turn one down, so it might be a good ice breaker. As soon as she opened the door, I held it out as a peace offering. She rolled her eyes but took the drink anyway.

I closed the front door and followed her into the living room. She sipped the drink quietly while watching me, waiting for me to say something. I shuffled my feet back and forth, not sure what to say or how to start.

"Well? Did you come over to bring me a drink and dance in my living room?"

"No…I uh... I... Sam, I'm sorry." I stuttered and finally blurted out.

She sat down on the couch and folded her arms.

I see I'm going to have to dig a little deeper. I sat in the armchair closest to the couch.

"Sam, I've been a terrible sister. I'm really sorry for the way I have behaved the last six months. I hope you can forgive me."

"Jo, you abandoned me when I needed you most. I was going through one of the most difficult things I have ever had to deal with, and you left me. I don't know how I can forgive you for that. I would have never done that to you! And all because you didn't agree with my choices? I know I did some fucked up shit and hurt a lot of people, but dammit you're my twin sister. We're supposed to have each other's backs regardless! And that half-ass apology is the best you can do?"

"You're right. Everything you said is true, and I'm not here to make excuses for my behavior but let me explain. Please?" I paused for a second, and she nodded for me to continue. "I've been angry and almost resentful for years. Things that I laugh about and say don't bother me are actually just eating away at me behind the scenes. Hell, I didn't even realize it myself until recently. I'm always in protective mode or fix-it mode so, when there are things I can't protect or fix, I retreat, I get angry and apparently I abandon my sister. I am so sorry for the way I neglected you. I wish I could take it back and do what we both needed me to do and that's have a conversation with you about everything. I wasn't just upset about your choices. I was also upset about our birthday. I felt like I was planning a party for you and not us planning a party together for each other. I also felt like, once again, our birthday turned into the Samantha show. I should have discussed this with you like an adult, and I'm so sorry. I mean it, Sam, I'm really, really sorry." By the time I finished my speech, I actually had tears in my eyes. Not again, I shook my head and looked away to get myself together.

"I didn't know." I could see from her body language that Sam had softened up a little. She uncrossed her arms and turned her body to face me more. "I didn't know any of that. I know I can be a brat sometimes, but I would never hurt you on purpose, Jo. As much as I care about others, I know I can also be very selfish. Jo, I wish you would have said something to remind me that the world doesn't revolve around me! I'm not gonna lie, and act like this changes everything else, but I think this is the perfect time for a fresh start and a new relationship. We need to be honest with each other from now on, regardless of how much it might hurt. It's the only way we can grow. Okay?"

"I completely agree, sis. Whatever it takes to make sure we're okay and that we stay that way. Besides, we're too old to be acting like this." I laughed a little as I stood up, pulling Sam off the couch for a hug.

She resisted a little at first as she rolled her eyes and snapped, "well, you started it."

"Really?" I bear-hugged her tight.

"Okay, okay, maybe you didn't start it. I'm sorry, too, Josie. I hate when we fight." She hugged me back almost as tight as I hugged her.

"I really missed you."

"I missed you too, sis." We stood there, just enjoying the embrace for a few minutes before we both let go and sat down. "So, what's up with you? Have you talked to Charlie lately? I haven't heard from her in a couple of weeks, which you know is weird for her. I even texted her this morning but no answer yet."

"Now that you mention it, I haven't heard from her either. Which I must admit, I hardly ever call her unless I need something. She usually reaches out to me. I really should do better with that."

"Same. I don't call that often either. It wasn't until Erica asked how she was doing that I realized I hadn't talked to her. We gotta do better, Sam. Life is too short, and God forbid something happens to any of us; we don't want to be sitting here trying to figure out when was the last time we talked to each other. So, with that being said, wanna do a road trip and go visit her?"

"I agree. Yeah, I'm down! When do you want to go? Just me and you or are we bringing Erica and…" She paused.

"Rose?" I offered.

My twin blushed and tried to hide her smile behind her hand before answering, "why would I bring Rose?"

"Girl bye." I replied with my lips twisted in a smirk.

"What?! Rose and I are...dating. We are exclusive, but we aren't in a relationship."

"Really? You don't seem thrilled about that, so I'm guessing that wasn't your decision?"

"No it wasn't, and no, I'm not thrilled about it. I kinda feel like she's punishing me for the whole Darrin situation. She's a little guarded, and it's confusing. She says she wants to be with me, and she's in love with me, but it doesn't feel the same."

I sat there in silence, trying to practice not offering my unsolicited opinion. It was clear, though, that Samantha was expecting me to say something. She stared at me, eyes big, and finally tilted her head to the side as if to say - 'hello?!'

"Do you want my opinion, Samantha?"

"Yes, Jo. Damn!"

"Don't do that. I'm practicing not jumping in without being asked. But since you asked, I hope you are ready for raw and uncut truth." I paused to be sure before I continued, Sam rolled her eyes and nodded her head yes. "I don't think it's fair of you to expect Rose to just jump back in 100% like nothing happened. You put her through a lot, and although I know you didn't intend for anyone to get hurt, everyone did. You strung both parties along for months. You decided to be with Darrin and even accepted that man's ring, knowing that you were really in love with her. The situation at the nightclub could have ended so much worse. Someone could have been physically hurt, not just emotionally. The fact that she is still willing to exclusively date, to me, shows how much she actually cares about you. She has every right to be a little guarded, Sam. I don't think she's intentionally trying to punish you, but maybe she's just trying to take it slow to protect herself. Considering all that, try to be as patient with her as she was with you. I hope that didn't come out too harsh." I finished softly because I didn't want to hurt or upset my sister. I wanted her to make better decisions, and I actually thought being with Rose was one of the best decisions she could make.

Sam sat quietly, and I was a little worried that she was upset with what I had said. After a few minutes, she finally said, "you're right. I'm being selfish and expecting things to go my way immediately. I'm really just happy she is still willing to give us a shot. So, if that means take it a little slow, then that's what I'll do!"

I was completely shocked, and I'm pretty sure my mouth was wide open. Samantha laughed, "Close your mouth, twin. So back to this trip. I think Charlie would be happy to see me and Rose back 'together' again, so if you're okay with it, I say let's make it a couples trip."

"Okay." I responded after I was able to find my voice again.

"Hold that thought, Erica's calling me. Hey, bestie." She answered her cell before I could say anything. "I'm actually sitting here talking to Jo right now. What time do you want to hang out? Jo, Erica wants to know are you guys getting together tonight?"

"Yeah she can come over after you guys hang out or tomorrow if she wants."

"Did you hear her? Okay. I'll call you in a little bit. Erica didn't know you were coming to talk to me?"

"No, I didn't tell her. Why? What she say?"

"Nothing, but I could tell she was surprised that you were here."

"Oh, okay. Well, if you guys have plans, then I'll head out." I started to get up.

"Don't be silly. I told her I'd call her back so we can finish talking."

"Okay." I smiled and settled back into the chair, thinking how good it felt to be catching up with my sister.

"So, anything new with you?" Samantha crossed her legs Indian style and propped her elbows on a pillow.

14. MICHAEL

God, please let my wife have a healthy pregnancy and birth. Please give me the strength to be there for my family in whatever capacity they need and continue leading them in Your direction Lord. These and all things I pray in Jesus' name. Amen.

I grabbed my car keys off the kitchen counter and met Charlie in the garage. I smiled at her and dangled the keys, "found them!"

"You're gonna make us late."

"We're not gonna be late, babe." I pulled her hand into my lap as I drove out of our development. Charlie was quiet the entire ride to the doctor's office as she had been most of the weekend. We checked in with the receptionist at the front desk and sat in the nearly empty waiting room. I held onto her hand while we waited. I'm sure she thought it was to comfort her, but it was just as much to comfort myself. After about 5 minutes, the nurse called us to the back. She took Charlie's vitals and put us in an exam room, assuring us that the doctor would be with us shortly. It wasn't long before someone tapped at the door.

Dr. Fuller came in smiling, "Michael, Charlotte, how are you?"

"Honestly, doc' we'll be better after we talk about our chances," I answered for both of us.

"Okay, let's get to it. As I mentioned on the phone, according to your blood work, you are about ten weeks, but I'd like to do an ultrasound as well. Your HCG levels are great, and I'm really optimistic about this pregnancy. So why don't we check for a heartbeat so Charlotte can start breathing again?" She smiled and grabbed Charlie's knee for reassurance.

I looked at my wife and saw her relax just a little. She leaned back on the table while Dr. Fuller pulled out everything she needed for the ultrasound. A few seconds later, we were listening to our baby's heartbeat and seeing the little peanut on the monitor. Charlie gasped out loud, and tears streamed down her cheeks. She smiled and squeezed my hand. I kissed her on the forehead as a couple of tears escaped from my eyes as well.

"I know you two may be fearful of getting excited about this pregnancy, but everything I see so far is pointing in the direction of a healthy pregnancy and birth. Charlotte, I need you to take it easy, not bed rest but just take it easy. If you have any pain, discomfort, spotting, anything that doesn't feel normal, I want you to call me immediately. I have alerted my staff and our answering service that you are a high-priority patient. I want to see you back in two weeks. That's the end of your first trimester. The front desk has your prescription for prenatal vitamins. Any questions?"

"We're really having a baby?" Those were the first words Charlie had spoken since we left home over an hour ago.

"Yes, Charlie. You're really having a baby." Dr. Fuller smiled and nodded, "Congratulations!"

"Thank you, Dr. Fuller." I stood up to shake her hand as she left the exam room. Charlie looked like she was still in shock. "You okay?" I sat back down next to her.

She looked at me with tears in her eyes, nodded, and smiled the biggest grin I had seen on her in days.

15. BRANDY

Fuck! I should have known that Tre couldn't be trusted! I'm never going to be able to get out of town now. I was barely able to sneak back by and get my car after Jo left the house. Thank God I keep a spare set of keys at the club.

Now that Jo is involved, there's no telling how long it will be before she turns me in. Clearly, no one believes that I'm innocent. I gotta get out of Atlanta ASAP. Maybe I can go by the new club and check the safe. The grand opening isn't for another week, but the vendor money should be there. I can grab that money and be long gone before anyone even notices that it's gone. Once I get to the West Coast, I'll check on Gloria. I'm sure she'll clear my name and tell them it was all just a misunderstanding and that I barely touched her. Just a little slap 'cause she kept asking all those damn questions about Rose. I mean first Samantha and then Gloria. What's this bitch got that's making all the females go crazy about her? She ain't even cute. Anyway, I bet Gloria won't make that mistake again. Just gonna boldly ask me about some other chick? She had me fucked up and thought I was stupid. Why they always think I'm stupid? Angie thought I was stupid too, but I showed her. They always try to play me, but in the end, I always win.

I parked at the end of the block to see if there were any cars at Kinky, our latest nightclub. There was a car in the parking lot, but it didn't look familiar. After about ten minutes, the car pulled off. I couldn't see who was driving, thanks to their tinted windows. I pulled my car closer but was unsure about parking in the lot.

I didn't want anyone riding by to know someone was there, but on the other hand, I didn't want to be seen running up the block. I parked as close as I could without being suspicious. After pulling my fitted cap down further and putting my hood on my head, I got out of the car, looked both ways, and darted across the street and into the parking lot. Within three minutes, I was in the back office opening the safe. I was slightly disappointed that there was only one band of 100-dollar bills and another band of twenties, but hey, it was better than the two hundred I currently had. I grabbed the two stacks and put them in the front pocket of my hoodie. I quickly closed the safe, hit the lights and alarm, and ran back to my car. The whole thing took me maybe 10 minutes. That was way too easy! I really should get on the road tonight, but I was exhausted, so I decided to get a room and head out at first light. Depending on how many times I need to stop for gas and breaks, I should be in Vegas in a day and a half. I always wanted to go to the West Coast. I think I've outgrown Atlanta anyway.

16. ROSE

I was sitting in my car in the hospital parking lot for the second time in two days, debating if I was actually going to go in this time. I don't know what I was afraid of or if I was afraid, or what the hell was wrong with me. I hadn't seen Gloria in over a decade, and while I knew I didn't have any feelings for her, for some reason, I still didn't want to be face to face with her. I smiled when my phone lit up with a message from Sam. Waking up in the bed next to her this morning was the best feeling ever. Sleeping on the couch together just wasn't quite the same.

I unlocked my phone to read her message.

```
Sam: Waking up next to you this morning was
amazing. We should do that more often.
Anyway, you'll never guess who came by this
morning and apologized? We actually had a
grown-up conversation, lol. It was great!
Anyway, how do you feel about a family road
trip? We were thinking about going to see
Charlie. I know she would love to see you.
I'll understand if you think it's too soon.
Call me later.
```

After that text from Sam, I decided not to go inside but to call instead to see what Gloria wanted from me. I called the mainline and asked to be connected to her room.

"Hello?"

"Gloria, it's Rose."

"Rose!" I could actually hear her smiling through the phone.

"Hey, Gloria. What's up?"

"Damn, I practically get beat into a coma, and that's all I get?"

"Well, what exactly do you want? I am not the investigator on your case anymore. There's not much else to say."

"After our history, you don't think there's anything else to say?"

"That's just it, Gloria. It's history. We haven't talked to or seen each other in years. What could we possibly have to talk about now?"

"I don't know. I just thought…"

"What did you think? That I would still be somewhere pining after you? Waiting for you to figure out what you wanted? I moved on a long time ago. I'm not that girl anymore."

"I know you've moved on. I've seen her. She's pretty, not as pretty as I normally am, but hey."

"What do you mean you've seen her? Where?"

"I came to the club looking for you. I was driving by Graphic one night and saw you at the door, so I went there a couple of nights later looking for you, but you weren't working that night. That's when I met Bran. She was sweet, and she said all the right things. We've been kicking it for almost a year now. She didn't really like me coming to the club, though, so my chances of running into you were slim. The last couple of months, I started trying to sneak in questions to figure out when you normally worked. But Bran was so jealous. I had to be strategic about my questions, so I didn't piss her off. Well, she finally got suspicious about all my questions. She wanted to know why I kept asking about you. When I couldn't give her an answer she liked, she spazzed out and punched me in the face. At first, I was shocked, but then I realized what had happened, and I hit her ass back. That's pretty much the last thing I remember. When I woke up, I saw your card in the bag with my belongings and asked the nurse to call you. I just wanted you to know that I came for you."

I could hear the tears in her voice. "I'm so sorry that this happened to you, and I promise you that Bran will pay. But as for us or whatever you thought you would find, that ship not only sailed, but it's sunk. There will never be a chance for us. Goodbye, Gloria."

"I know what the doctor said, Michael. I was there too."

"So, you're going on bed rest for the remainder of your pregnancy even though she said it's not necessary?"

"I didn't say the remainder, and I'm not on bed rest. I just lightened my workload for the next two weeks until we go back to the doctor."

"And after that?"

"I don't know! I just want to make sure our baby is safe!" I yelled and slammed my favorite mug on the counter.

"Charlie, I understand that my, Luv, but I don't want you to isolate yourself away from your friends and family for the next 6 to 7 months, especially if it's not necessary. Your mental health is just as important."

"I'm not crazy!"

"I didn't say…forget it. Have you even called your sisters back? They've both been calling and texting for days. Are you planning on telling them soon? You know what? Never mind, 'cause you're going to do what you want to do anyway. I'm late for work. I love you." Michael kissed me on the forehead and walked out of the kitchen. I heard the garage door slam a few minutes later.

I sat down on one of the barstools in front of my island. Placing my hands on my stomach, I sat there in quiet meditation and prayer until my teapot whistled, startling me out of my moment. After making a cup of my favorite tea, I retired to the couch with my laptop and a blanket. I wanted to text Michael to apologize but couldn't bring myself to do it, yet. I knew he was scared, too, and only wanted what was best for me and the baby. I decided to send him an Edible Arrangement as an apology until I got the nerve up to text him later. I couldn't have my hubby mad at me, especially right now, since I didn't want to tell anyone about the baby until after my next appointment. He was all I had. He was all I've ever wanted. After setting up the delivery to his office, I changed my mind and sent him a text, too.

I smiled, remembering just how blessed I was that God created that man for me. I checked my schedule to see what showings I could pass off to one of the other agents for the rest of the week. I kept a few for myself just but spaced them out so as not to have more than two to three in the same day. After reaching out to some new clients and leads, I got up to make myself something to eat. I guess I'll call the twins back after I eat or maybe after I take a nap. I wasn't necessarily avoiding them, but since I didn't want to tell them about the baby yet, it would be easier if I could just wait to talk to them. On the other hand, if I don't get back to them soon, then they'll get worried and start calling Michael. Ugh, forget it, I picked up my cell phone and called Sam. She sent me to voicemail and followed up with a text.

Sam: Hey sissy. Where you been? I'm in a meeting. Call you later.

Charlie: Just been busy with work. I'll be around later. Call when you can.

Okay, guess I'll try Jo.

"Damn Charlie, I thought I was going to have to send out an APB for you. What's up? You good?" She answered on the first ring.

"I'm fine, Jo. You guys are so dramatic." I laughed.

"I'm not dramatic. It's just not like you to go MIA like that. I haven't heard from you in weeks."

"It hasn't been weeks. Okay, maybe ONE week. But maybe if you picked up the phone sometimes and called me then-"

"You're right. I apologize, and I promise to do better with that. Did you get my message? We were thinking about coming to visit this weekend. Is that cool?"

"Umm not this weekend. I already have a lot of showings scheduled. How about at the end of the month? That'll give me time to make sure me and Michael's schedule is clear."

"Aight, that sounds good."

"Who all is coming? You and Erica?"

"I'm pretty sure Sam is coming too. When I mentioned it to her, she seemed pretty excited about it. I'll give them both the date later tonight."

"Great. So, it sounds like you two are back on good terms?"

"Yeah, we are. I apologized to her-"

I cut Josephine off mid-sentence, "YOU apologized?"

Jo chuckled a little, "Yes, I apologized. I realized how much I hurt her and that I was in the wrong. I guess both of your sisters are still growing up."

"Josephine, I'm really proud of you. There is nothing wrong with admitting you are wrong or continuing to grow. That should be a continuous part of life."

"Charlie, I don't think I ever apologized to you."

"For what?" I asked, genuinely confused.

"For all that I put you through after mom and dad died."

"Jo, that was a rough time for all of us. You don't-"

"Please, let me finish," she cut me off.

"Okay."

"Yes, I know it was a rough time for all of us, and I know I didn't make it any easier. But you never gave up on me. You could have sent me away or put me out, but you continued to show up for me even when I didn't deserve it. So just in case I've never said it before, I'm sorry and thank you. I know I wouldn't be half of who I am today if it were not for you."

"Jo, I could never give up on you. You are my sister. Not only that, I knew who you would be, even when you didn't know. I will always be your biggest cheerleader. Right, wrong, or indifferent, you are still mine."

"So, what's new with you guys? How is my beautiful niece?"

Jo was never one for praise and attention. So, it was not surprising for her to quickly change the subject.

"Nothing new over here. You know the usual. Danielle is great. She's thinking about joining the debate team."

"Word? That's what's up! She's following in her auntie's footsteps."

"Well, she definitely got the arguing gene naturally!"

We laughed and talked on the phone for at least an hour. I didn't even realize how much I missed talking to her.

She promised she would call more often, and I promised to do the same. I couldn't wait to tell her and Sam about their new little niece or nephew.

I pulled up next to Jo's motorcycle parked at the same park where we had our first date. I thought this would be a good place to meet to talk. She wanted to explain what her breakdown was all about from the other night, and I needed to tell her that Sadie had been down the hall sleeping that night. I was right on time, but of course, Jo was early. Knowing her, she was setting up at our usual spot. I said a quick prayer that she would understand before getting out of my car.

Once I reached the top of the hill, I could see Jo lying down on a blanket under 'our' tree. She looked like she might be sleeping, and as I got closer, I could tell she was asleep. I don't know why the thought crossed my mind that I could surprise her because as soon as I reached the edge of the blanket, she said in her usual sexy tone, "don't even think about it."

"Think about what, baby?" I asked innocently right before she sat up, grabbed me around my waist, and pulled me down next to her.

She did it so quickly and smoothly. I didn't even have a chance to react. Jo leaned over, pressing the top half of her body on mine, and kissed me on the lips.

"Hey," she smiled.

"Hey. What was all of that for?"

"Why I gotta have a reason to kiss my girl? It can't be because I love you? Or I miss you? Or I'm happy that you're mine?" She still had me pinned under her body, and I could smell my favorite cologne, instant turn on.

"Well, I love all those reasons, but if you don't move, we will never get to the reason we're supposed to be here." I pulled her down for another kiss and then gently pushed her back.

"I guess." She reluctantly sat up, and I followed suit, sitting up next to her and resting my head on her shoulder.

"Babe, we tight, right?" Jo asked, staring off into space.

"Of course, we are. Why would you ask me that?" I asked, guilty, wondering if she knew about Sadie.

"I know we've only been together a year, but it feels like a lifetime, and I want to make it forever."

"Whoa, Jo…." I said nervously.

"Chill, I'm not proposing right now," she laughed, "I just want you to know my intentions and what I want for us. Is that what you want?"

I paused for half a second, "Yes. That's what I want for us too."

"I have to tell you about something I did when I was in college. It's not something I am proud of, but I don't want to ever keep secrets from you."

"Is this what you were upset about the other night?"

"It was part of it."

"Okay. I have to tell you something too, and I kind of want to go first if that's cool. Otherwise, I might chicken out. Do you mind?"

"Of course not, baby. What's up?" I could feel her looking down at me.

"I met with Sadie the other day."

"For what now?"

"And she stayed the night at my house the night you came by."

Jo's body immediately tensed up to the point that the arm my head was resting on felt like a rock. "I think maybe you should explain before I jump to conclusions." She said through clenched teeth.

I sat up straight and moved so that I was sitting across from her.

"It's not what you think. She was blowing up my phone with calls and texts saying that it was an emergency, then she asked me to meet her to talk. When I got there, she was crying. She informed me that she had just come out to her mother. Her mom basically disowned her on the spot and forbade her from seeing her younger sister. She told her that she was dead to her. She was a complete mess, babe, and I couldn't in good conscience leave her alone like that. She said she doesn't really have any other friends or family here. So, I asked her to come back to my place that night just to make sure she was okay. I called and texted you so we could talk about it, but that was the day you were dealing with your emergency. I just wanted to be sure she was safe. She stayed in the guest room. Jo, please tell me you understand."

She was silent for several minutes before responding, "I understand. I don't necessarily agree with your decision to bring her home, but I trust you, and I know that you wouldn't do anything to hurt us. Have you talked to her since then? How is she?"

I didn't realize I was holding my breath until she finished talking. "While I realized how this could look, I really did just want to help her. There are so many in our community that lose their family and even their lives after coming out, and I didn't want Sadie to be another statistic. I've talked to her a couple of times, and she seems to be holding up okay."

"You're right about that, and I really do understand why you did it. I'm not mad, baby. Your heart and compassion are just two of the many reasons I love you. So, what's the plan to continue to help her? Cause even though I understand, she ain't moving in!" She smiled at me and grabbed my hand, kissing it. I smiled back, happy to have this out in the open. She was right; I didn't want to keep secrets from her either.

"Well, there's no need for all of that, crazy. You know Sadie has her own place. I made it clear to her that the sexual part of our relationship was over but that I would like to be there for her. She was okay with that, and we found a support group that meets once a week. I want to go with her, at least for the first couple of weeks. What you think?"

"I think that's a good idea. As long as she knows that we are both done with all the other stuff, then I want to help out any way I can, babe. Regardless of our history with her, I don't want anything to happen to her. She's a sweet girl. Let me know what you need, and I got you."

"Thank you, Jo. That means a lot to me."

"Thank you for telling me."

"You're welcome, babe. So, what's your big, dark secret?" I grinned at her.

"You know I've been friends with Tre and Bran for a long time, right?"

"Yeah, since elementary school?" I asked, wondering what they had to do with her secret.

"I met them in second grade. They were already friends when we moved into the neighborhood, but we all still instantly clicked. The fact that we stayed friends through to adulthood is kind of rare these days. We've been there for each other through all types of loss. Just like I went through my rebellious time when my parents died, so did Bran when her granddad passed away. Her grandparents raised her, and she was really close to her grandfather. The difference between us is that I eventually got my shit together while Bran still seemed to struggle. She always had anger issues, but they got worse after Pop Saul died. Almost every fight I've gotten into in my life has been because of Brandy. She ended up having to repeat senior year, which made her even angrier. The fact that me and Tre were going to college and leaving her behind drove her crazy. She started dating this girl, Angie. They were so, toxic. They argued like crazy, mostly about the fact that Angie had just broken up with a guy right before they got together. Bran constantly wanted Angie to compare the relationships and basically stroke Bran's ego. Anyway, about two months into them going out, Angie found out she was three months pregnant. Anyone with common sense could count and knew that she didn't cheat on Bran. She was pregnant before they got together; she just didn't know it. Bran didn't really have common sense, though. They got into a huge fight, which turned physical. Bran claimed she only slapped her once, but whatever happened, Angie fell down the stairs. Bran didn't stay to make sure she was okay. She left and went to play basketball with some friends. Angie drove herself to the hospital and ended up losing her baby. Even after all that, Bran didn't change. She blamed the whole thing on Angie and said that's what she got for cheating on her. Angie wanted to go to the police and press charges, so of course now Bran was scared. She called Tre, who in turn called me. Tre asked me to see if I could talk to Angie and convince her not to go to the police. I ended up paying Angie off to be quiet." Jo paused to gauge my reaction so far. I was speechless. I didn't know what to say, and since I wondered if there was more to the story, I just kept quiet. After about a minute of silence, Jo continued.

"I didn't know what else to do. I didn't want my friend to go to jail, so I gave her thirty grand and bought her a plane ticket to New York. She said she had a sister there and wanted to pursue modeling."

"Thirty grand?! Jo, where did you get that kind of money? You were still in college." I blurted out.

"It was part of my money from when my parents died. We were given small payments up until our twenty-fifth birthday, which is when we received the rest. The money I gave her was what I had saved up. To my knowledge, Bran never heard from Angie again, and she agreed to go to anger management classes. She only went for about a month, though. I was so disappointed with myself for what I had done that I started slipping into a depression. My sophomore year, I begged Charlie to let me go overseas for a year. It was like a foreign exchange program. I ended up staying for two years. I returned and finished my senior year. Bran seemed to have matured a lot while I was gone. Even Tre said she was doing really well and had gotten her anger under control."

"Jo, I don't know what to say…"

"Before you say anything, there's more. The day I told you I was dealing with an emergency, it was the most recent Brandy situation. Tre asked me to come by her crib early that morning. When I got there, she told me that Bran was hiding out at her crib because she had beat up her current girlfriend so badly that she left her unconscious. In typical Bran fashion, she lied and said the girl beat herself up. Who the hell does that? Bran didn't even know if the girl was alive. When we went inside to confront Bran, she had run out the back door."

"Oh my God! What in the hell?! So she's out here on the run? What about her girlfriend?" I couldn't believe Jo was so calm about this situation.

"She's okay. I was able to find out that much."

"So, what are you planning to do? You're not going to help her again?" Although I phrased it as a question, in my mind, it was a statement.

"No, I'm not helping her again, babe. This was just too much. She literally beat this chick into a coma. I can't be a part of that. I just wanted you to know the full story from me about everything in case it comes out at some point. I don't know what Brandy is capable of anymore. I'm just trying to figure out what to do."

"We will figure it out together. You are not in this alone. And no, I'm not judging you for a decision you made when you were young. You did what you thought was right to help your friend. Now you have to do what is right. Period. What do you think about calling Rose?"

"I was thinking about that. Maybe she can at least try to make sure Brandy is brought in safely. I can't really ask for anything more than that. I'll see if I can meet up with her tomorrow."

"I'm sure she'll do whatever she can, baby, just talk to her."

Ugh, why did I agree to meet Darrin tonight? I could have just as easily mailed his stuff to him. On the other hand, it's the least I could do after everything else. Five minutes isn't going to kill me. He arrived at my condo promptly at 6:30, carrying a couple of boxes of what I assumed was left of our relationship.

"Hey," I don't know why I felt so shy all of a sudden. This man had been my world for years.

"Hola bella dama."

"I see you've been working on your Spanish." I smiled.

"I have. Do you mind if I use your bathroom?" He asked immediately after putting the boxes on the floor next to my couch.

"Go ahead. Can I get you something to drink?" I was hoping he wouldn't be here that long, but I still had to be polite.

"A beer would be nice if you have one." He yelled back as he headed down the hall to the half bathroom.

Dammit, I thought to myself. I grabbed him a beer from the six-pack Jo had leftover. God knows I can't stand the stuff. I decided to pour a glass of wine for myself too. If he was staying for a minute, I needed to make it bearable. By the time he came back down the hall, I was already sitting on the couch, and his beer was on the coffee table across from me in front of one of my armchairs.

"Thanks," he picked up the beer and took a drink, "How have you been?"

"I've been good. How about you?"

"Pretty good. Just sent the last of my stuff over to Madrid. I'm leaving in a couple of days."

"That sounds exciting!"

"Kind of. It's still bittersweet."

"Darrin, please." I cut him off. Here we go again, I thought.

"I'm not here to argue, Samantha. It was just a statement, that's all."

"Oh, sorry."

"Don't apologize. I know the last couple of months weren't easy on either of us. I appreciate you going to counseling, though."

"Of course. I mean, it was the least I could do. Darrin, I know I have said this before, but I can't stress enough that this wasn't about you. I needed to figure out what it was that I felt I was missing."

"I understand that now. I do have one question, though. Why didn't you think you could come to me? Why couldn't you tell me how you were feeling or that you felt you were missing something? Maybe we could have worked through it together, Samantha. You made the decision for and without me."

"I don't know. Since I struggled with accepting it, I just assumed you wouldn't understand or accept it either. I'm sorry I didn't trust you with that part of me. Do you think that would have changed anything?"

"Maybe. I don't know. Maybe we could have experimented together. I might have enjoyed having two women in my bed." He laughed to lighten the mood.

"Haha, real funny. You and I both know that's not our thing. Besides, I highly doubt Rose would have gone for that." Shit! That slipped out.

"Yeah, good old Rose."

"Sorry, I didn't mean-"

"No, it's fine. It's only natural that her name would come up. I mean, you two are together, right?"

"No, we're not together." I sipped my wine, wishing it was a little stronger.

"Hmmm okay. So did I have a lot of stuff to pack?" He stood up abruptly.

"Darrin, you don't have to go." I stood up too.

"I do. I'm meeting my mom for dinner."

"Oh. Well, your box is by the door. You didn't have a lot."

"Cool, thanks." We were standing by the front door. "Can I have a hug?"

"Yes."

His embrace was so strong yet gentle, kind of like him. When he finally let go, he looked into my eyes, grabbed my face, and kissed me, "I will always love you, Samantha." It sounded like his voice cracked a little, but he turned away quickly, swooped up his box, and was out of the door before I could respond.

"I will always love you too, Darrin," I said out loud to myself as tears streamed down my face.

"Hey. What's up, Jo?"

"What's up? Are you available to meet up?"

"Not today. I just pulled up to the precinct. Tonight's my last night on the overnight shift, and tomorrow morning I have a personal training client. You okay?"

"Yeah, I'm good. Just need to talk to you about something important."

"I'm going to be at Sam's tomorrow night cooking dinner. If you want, we can meet before then."

"Speaking of Sam. When were you going to tell me you two were back together?"

"My bad, man. Shit has been really hectic lately. Plus, she told me you two made up, so I knew you knew."

"Man, you know my girl can't hold water, so I knew when you stayed over that night." Jo laughed into the phone.

"Wooooow!" I laughed too, "Matter' fact, why don't you and Erica come join us tomorrow? It would be good for us all to hang out, and we'll get a chance to talk."

"Okay, that sounds good. It has been a little minute since we've all been together. Maybe now shit can get back to normal!"

"Yeah, whatever that is! I'll see you tomorrow. I'm about to go into the precinct."

"Aight, see you tomorrow."

I wonder if Jo knows about Bran. I hope she's not expecting no damn favor from me when it comes to her. I guess I'll find out tomorrow. I shot Sam a quick text reminding her that I wouldn't be available until tomorrow and that I had invited Jo and Erica for dinner. She texted back a thumbs-up emoji. That wasn't like her. I was about to call her when she sent a kissy face too. That was a little better, but...

"Hathaway, you coming in, or you plan on spending the shift sitting in your car?"

"Real funny, Morris." I laughed as I got out of my car and pocketed my cell phone. We walked together, discussing how it was a full moon, and we were hoping it wouldn't be a crazy night.

I got up from my nap and checked my phone, a little surprised that Samantha hasn't texted. She usually sends some cute little message or something for me to wake up to. That brought me back to her emoji only text from last night. I know it's easy to misinterpret a text, but that just wasn't like her. I decided to call her to discuss our dinner plans.

"Hello," she answered on the third ring.

"Hey, gorgeous. How's your day going?"

"It's going good. It's actually been pretty chill. I was thinking about cutting out early."

"That's good. If you're able to get off early, then I could start cooking. Did you decide what you want to eat, babe?"

"Not really. What you think about sparking up the grill? It's such a nice day out. Maybe we can all sit on the patio?"

"Perfect. I can make some shrimp and chicken kabobs. Anything else you need me to grab? I'm about to get dressed and head out."

"Nah, whatever you decide to make is fine. If you get to my place before me, you know where the key is, so just let yourself in. I'll get out of here as soon as I can."

"Okay, I'll see you soon."

I got to the condo before her, so I let myself in with her hideaway key. I put the dragon roses that I picked up from the florist in a vase and turned on some music before I started prepping dinner. I must have been in a zone because I didn't hear Samantha come in.

"Dammit, woman! You almost gave me a heart attack!" She was standing in the doorway to the kitchen, watching me.

"Some detective you are," she teased.

"Maybe you're just better at being sneaky," I shot back.

"Hmmm, I'm going to change into something comfortable, and then I'll help."

"I got this. You go change and relax."

"Okay."

She returned a few minutes later and hugged me from behind, resting her head on my back.

"What's wrong, baby?" I asked as I pulled her around to face me.

"Nothing. It's just been a long week. I'm happy you're here."

"I'm happy to be here. Since I don't have to work tomorrow, I can stay over if you want."

"That's up to you."

"Since when? Any other time you're demanding that I'm here or that you come to my place. You don't want to spend the night with me?" I teased.

"I do. I'm just wondering how long you're going to have me on restriction."

"Restriction? Oh, we're back on this again."

"It's just a question, Rose. Not an unreasonable one either."

"No, it's not unreasonable, but we just started back dating. I'm just asking for a little time. We're both in a bit of a vulnerable place."

"Isn't the point to be vulnerable with each other?"

"You know that's not what I mean, Sam. Are you trying to pick a fight with me?"

"No, but I have a right to know what I'm signing up for."

I couldn't help but laugh a little at that statement, considering who was saying it, but I swore to myself I wouldn't throw the past in her face.

"So that's funny to you." She had her hands on her hips, and I couldn't help but think how cute she was when she was angry. To be honest, I wanted to put her ass on the counter and have her for dinner, but something in me was still holding back.

"I'm sorry, I wasn't laughing at you. You do have the right to know what you're signing up for. I just need some time to think about it. The truth is, I don't have an answer myself."

"Sure, Rose. You can think about it." She brushed past me so she could storm out of the kitchen.

"Sam, please don't be like that."

"What's wrong with you?" Jo asked as she entered the kitchen with Erica right behind her.

"Hi, Rose! Bye, Rose!" Erica yelled and waved as Sam grabbed her hand and led her out of the kitchen. A few minutes later, we heard a door shut upstairs.

"Damn, what was that all about? Do we need to take a rain check?" Jo laughed as she gave me a quick hug.

"Bruh, trust you don't want to know!"

"You right! Let me grab a beer."

"Oh, I forgot to buy some."

"That's cool. I left a six-pack over here. Damn, somebody started drinking without me." Jo pulled out the carton, and there were a couple of beers missing already.

"Well, don't look at me! I don't really drink that brand like that, and you know Sam can't stand beer, so I don't know what to tell you."

"Maybe I drank more than I thought. Shit, I don't know." Jo offered me a beer and sat down at the island. "Do you need help with anything?"

"Nah, I've got everything prepared already. Want to go out on the patio? That way, we can talk, and I can watch the food too."

"Yeah, let's do that."

I put the kabobs and vegetables on the grill and sat down across from Jo. "So, what's up? What did you want to talk about?"

"It's about Bran. She Ummm, she uhhhh…" Jo seemed at a loss for words, so I decided to jump in to help her.

"She beat a woman unconscious and then fled the scene, leaving the woman for dead?"

"You know?!"

"I am a detective, Jo."

"I know that. I just didn't think you knew about this. You didn't say anything."

"It's an open investigation. There isn't much that I can say."

"I understand."

"Do you have information that could help the case?" I was trying to make it clear that this would be handled strictly as business.

"Not really."

"Then there isn't much more to talk about. Do you know where she's hiding? Are you helping to hide her? Don't put me in a position between my job and you, Jo."

"Hell no, I'm not hiding her. Besides, I wouldn't ask you to do that. I was only going to ask if you could make sure she's brought in safe."

"I'm not the investigator on the case, so it's not much I can do either way, but it really would be best for her if she just turned herself in."

"Yeah, she's definitely not going to do that. When Tre told me what she had done, we went to confront her together, and she ran. I have no idea where she could be. I have security at all of the clubs on high alert, and I even put trackers in some of the cash in our safes. Just in case she's stupid enough to lift some cash."

"Nice move. So, I'm guessing nothing has moved? She hasn't been seen?"

"Nope. She went to Tre's asking for cash, and when Tre got suspicious as to why she needed so much, Brandy made up a story about what had happened. We haven't seen or heard from her since she ran out the back door to keep from facing me. If I had known what I was walking into, I would have called you first."

"I appreciate that. It's out of my hands now, though. I'm curious, what did she say happened?"

"She claimed she only hit the girl once and the rest she did to herself. Hold on a second. My club manager has called three times. It must be urgent. Hello? Damn. How much? Did you check the security footage? Okay, no, no need to call the police. I'll handle it. Well, she has been seen. We have a club that's not open yet. Looks like Bran hit the safe the other night. She got at least five grand."

"Shit. Any chance you had a tracker on that money?"

"I didn't even think about that place, so I doubt it. Let me check with my head of security, though. Maybe she did."

"Okay, I'll wait to call it in until you find out. You want another beer?" I stood up to go inside.

"Yeah, thanks, man." Jo handed me her empty bottle.

I almost threw the bottles in the trash then I remembered how Samantha was always fussing about recycling. I pulled open the recycling drawer, and there was both an empty beer and wine bottle right on top. Okay, so who's been drinking beer? I thought to myself. I grabbed a bottle and handed it out the door to Jo. Since she was talking on the phone, I assumed with her security, I decided to go talk to Sam. Maybe Erica had gotten her to calm down some. Even though Sam's bedroom door was closed, I could still hear her and Erica talking as I walked down the hallway.

"The question is, are you going to tell Rose?"

"I don't know. I feel like it's going to cause more problems. It already feels like she's punishing me."

"I think not telling her would definitely cause a problem, Samantha. If you are trying to build a relationship, then you need to build trust. How can she trust you if you are hiding things from her? I don't think she's intentionally punishing you either. You gotta stop being so dramatic, friend. At the end of the day, you have to accept that you hurt her and cut her a little slack. Try to be a little more patient. Do you really love her?"

"Of course, I do! I love her, and I'm in love with her, Erica. I know I hurt her, and I don't want to ever put her through that again. So, you're right, I'm going to tell her about Darrin AND be more patient. I hate when you're right!"

I felt guilty for eavesdropping on their conversation, but I really hoped that Sam would take Erica's advice about whatever secret she wasn't sure about telling me. I waited in the hall a few minutes before knocking on the door.

"Come in!" Sam yelled.

"Hey, can I borrow my girl for a minute?" I asked Erica.

"Of course! Let me go check on my boo." She hopped off the bed.

"I think she's on the phone," I said as she passed by and patted me on the shoulder for reassurance. Hell, even she knew her best friend was a trip. "Babe, can we talk?"

"Yes, but me first. I have to tell you something. You're not going to like it."

"Okay, I'm listening." I sat on her bed, facing her.

"Darrin asked if he could come by and bring my personal belongings that I left at his house and also to pick up his stuff from me. So, he came by last night and stayed for a little while. We talked and had a drink together. As always, he referred back to what happened with him, and I really felt like I owed him that closure. I told him that it wasn't about him. It was about me. Anyway, that's not really relevant. When he left, he asked for a hug. I didn't think it would be a problem, but afterward, he kissed me. No tongue or anything like that, just a simple goodbye kiss." She stopped and looked anxious as she waited for me to respond.

"That's it?"

"Yes, that's all. Nothing else happened. I didn't even kiss him back. It happened so fast, and then he left. I honestly wasn't sure if I should even tell you because I didn't want to upset you, and it meant absolutely nothing to me."

"Well, I appreciate you for being honest with me. I get that it wasn't easy, but I want us always to be honest with each other. That's the only way this is going to work."

"You're not mad?"

"No. You guys were together for years, Sam. You both needed that closure. I trust and believe you that the kiss didn't mean anything to you."

"Really?"

I chuckled a little, "Yes, Samantha. I will always believe you unless you give me a reason not to. Okay?"

She smiled, "okay. So, your turn."

"I wanted to apologize."

"For what?"

"For not truly letting go of our past and being present for our future. If we are going to truly move forward, then I have to be able to let all of that go, including the pain. I can't say that I trust you if I'm still operating from a guarded place. So, I'm completely opening myself up to you, to us."

"Rose, that means so much to me. I know I hurt you, and I can never apologize enough for that, but I want to do and be better. You make me want those things. I want to give us a real chance. I am completely, madly in like, lust and love with you."

"All of that, huh?" I laughed.

"Yes, all of that." Sam slid closer to me, leaned over, and kissed me. "So, you gonna let me in those pants now?"

I pulled her into my lap and slid my hands up her shirt. "I think that can be arranged. Not tonight, though. I have to go into the precinct about a case."

"I thought you were off tonight," Samantha whined and then moaned as I licked her neck.

"I am, but I need to give them some information. I might be coming back, but I don't like to make promises that I don't know if I can keep."

Now it was my turn to moan a little. Sam was nibbling my ear. "Maybe I'll see if I can just call in the information without having to go in."

"Okay, good." She hopped off my lap, gave me a quick peck, and headed towards the door.

"Oh, okay, you got me." I got off the bed and followed her out of the room and downstairs.

"It's a good thing somebody was down here paying attention to the food, or we'd be ordering pizza for dinner!" Erica yelled when we entered the kitchen.

"Thanks, Erica. I appreciate it."

Jo came in from outside and motioned towards the living room so we could speak in private.

"Why don't you ladies sit outside, and we'll make the plates and serve you?" I asked as I gently eased Sam and Erica towards the door. Once they were outside and the door was closed, I asked, "so what's up?"

"My head of security did put a tracker in the money at the new club. She just turned it on, and it looks like she's headed west."

"Yesss! I gotta call the investigator on the case. Are you able to share the tracking information?"

"Yeah, just let me know where to send it."

"Text or email it to me. Do you mind fixing the plates while I make this call?"

"No problem. Go do what you need to do."

I nodded and walked into the living room. My work phone was in my duffel bag by the door. I stepped into Samantha's office and closed the door while I called Detective Moore. I told him I would send over the tracking information, and he told me he would let me know when they got her. I walked onto the patio, smiling as I sat down to join everyone.

"Does that smile mean you don't have to go into work tonight?" Sam leaned in close to ask.

"Mmhmm, that's exactly what it means." I kissed her softly.

"Would you two cut it out? You're worse than us!" Jo exclaimed.

"No one's worse than us, babe." Erica laughed.

"Yeah, you right."

We laughed, drank, and ate until it got dark. Then we turned on the patio lights and sat a little longer. Sam was a little tipsy by this time and was sexting me dirty messages about how bad she wanted me. I tried my best to be a good guest hostess to Jo and Erica, but I really wanted them to go already. Then I would fulfill my fantasy of having Samantha for dessert, right on the kitchen counter. Samantha eventually got up and started clearing the dishes. A few minutes later, Erica went to help her. I thanked Jo again for help with Bran and told her I would do my best to keep her posted. I walked her inside, clearing the last of the bottles off the table. Samantha was at the sink washing dishes, and Erica was putting the leftovers in containers.

"Erica, I'll finish that."

"I'm done. You guys have a good night, and don't do anything we wouldn't do." She winked at Sam, who rolled her eyes.

"Well shit, babe, that's not much!" Jo laughed and smacked her on the butt as she walked by. "Night, twin!" She yelled at Sam and dapped me on her way out the kitchen.

"Night, twin!" Sam yelled back.

I walked them to the door and locked up. Sam was still washing dishes, so I came up behind her, wrapped my arms around her waist, and nuzzled her neck.

"I'm almost done, and we can go upstairs. Unless you want to sit down here for a while?"

"Whatever you want to do," I answered softly while my hands traveled slowly towards her thighs. I was really happy that she had changed into a skirt when she came home, and I pulled it up to her waist. "Turn around," I demanded. Once she was facing me, I dropped to my knees and pulled her panties down. She lifted one leg and then the other, allowing me to take them off. I put her right leg on my shoulder and dove into her sweetness, tongue first. Samantha gasped out loud, and after a couple of licks, she was grabbing my head. I lifted her up and sat her on the counter so that I could continue licking and sucking at her clit. It wasn't long before she was holding my head in place and calling my name.

"Oh my God! Rose! Right there!"

I smiled and hummed a little, which I knew she could feel as well. Then I stopped abruptly to run to the fridge. She was catching her breath so I was back before she got a chance to protest. When she felt the ice between her legs, she called out again. The cold prolonged her orgasm by another several minutes. Judging by the amount of juice on my face, it was safe to say she was satisfied. I eased her legs off my shoulders and stood up.

"You okay?" I asked

"Not really."

"What's wrong?" I was worried.

"Only one of us has two sets of wet lips."

She pulled my t-shirt over my head, jumped down from the counter, took my hand, and walked me to the living room. After loosening my sweats, she pulled them down and pushed me to the couch. I don't even remember her taking my pants or underwear completely off but next thing I knew, she was between my legs. She looked me in my eyes as she flicked her tongue over my clit. I was trying my best not to break eye contact and throw my head back in ecstasy, but damn, it was hard. She must have taken that as a challenge because she switched up the rhythm and technique. I wasn't expecting that, and I let out a moan before I could stop myself. Pleased with herself, Sam intensified her tongue strokes.

I couldn't hold back anymore. I yelled 'Fuck' and locked my legs as the orgasm rocked my body. It had been way too long since that release. I had to pull Samantha off the floor, or else she would have kept going. She was smiling like a Cheshire Cat, overly pleased with herself. She straddled my lap and kissed me, the taste of us both driving me crazy.

"Give me a minute to catch my breath, and we're going again," I said against her lips.

"Mmmm. I can do this all night, baby." She kissed my neck.

"That's the plan." I flipped her off my lap and onto her back.

I walked to my car from the gas station as calm as I could, trying not to make eye contact with the two Texas Rangers talking in the parking lot, all while not trying to look guilty. After all, I know there's no way they're looking for me. No one knows where I'm headed, and I've been mainly taking back roads the whole time. Remembering all of that, I immediately calmed my nerves and even nodded and smiled at them on my way to the car. After getting inside, I sat for a minute, sipping my water and opening the new burner phone I had just purchased. I had tossed my cell phone a couple of exits back, just to be safe.

A few minutes later, I was cruising along with the light traffic, my windows down, and my music blaring. I looked in my rearview mirror and saw the Rangers several cars behind me. They didn't have their lights on, and they weren't speeding as if they were trying to catch anyone. I didn't think anything about it and kept cruising along. A few minutes later, they turned on the sirens and sped up. The cars behind me pulled over to let them pass, and for a second, I thought, maybe they're going to pass me as I started to slow down and switch lanes. But when I changed lanes, so did they, and I realized they were after me. I panicked and quickly sped back up. I pushed my car to limits I didn't know it could go. Before I knew it, I was going well over 100, switching from lane to lane in between traffic. The adrenaline pumping through my veins had me feeling as if I was flying. Dammit, I knew I shouldn't have gotten on I-40!! Maybe there's an exit coming up, and I can jump off and lose them in the busier city traffic. I picked up the burner phone and dialed Jo's number. Fuck, she sent me to voicemail.

"Jo, it's me, Bran. Listen, I know you don't believe my story, but I promise Gloria set me up. I'll admit I slapped her once, but that's it. She did the rest of that stuff to herself, Jo. I know my history, but she's really crazy. She was asking all these questions about

Rose. Like maybe she knew her. Either way, you gotta help me clear my name. I'm in Texas, and they're trying to get me. I can't go to jail, Jo. Call me back and tell me what to do!"

I was flashing my lights and blowing my horn at any car that wasn't moving out of my way fast enough and driving so fast I almost didn't see the sign that said the next exit was two miles away. I whipped past a few more cars and sped up so I could jump in front of a tractor-trailer before I missed the exit. After I cleared the truck, I saw the Tahoe, but it was too late for either of us to do anything. I hit the front and flipped upside down. Damn, why didn't I just stay and talk to Jo in the first place?"

22. ERICA

"Thanks again for coming with me to my first meeting, Erica."

"You're welcome, Sadie. I told you I would be here for you."

"And you're sure Jo is going to be okay with us spending all of this time together?"

"She is okay with it. I told her everything, and she is very supportive."

"Oh, that's good. Want to grab a bite to eat?"

I checked my watch and my phone before responding, "Yeah, we can do that."

"I know the perfect spot. You can ride with me!"

"No, I'll drive my car. Text me the address."

"Okay."

After we ordered, I asked Sadie if she had heard anything from her mom.

"No, not since that day."

"Have you tried to call her?"

She shook her head no and looked down at her hands.

"Hey, it's okay. I was just asking. We don't have to talk about it if you don't want to."

"Thank you. So have you and Jo brought in a new third yet?"

I choked on the water I was drinking.

"Ummm, so I know I said we were 'friends,' but this isn't a conversation that we will be having, like ever."

"But why? I mean, it's not like I don't know or haven't literally been there. I'm just curious as to who you replaced me with." Sadie smiled mischievously.

"Yeah, like I said, not a conversation that we will be having. When is your next meeting?"

She rolled her eyes and pouted before answering, "there's one on Friday. Can you make it?"

"I'll have to get back to you. I don't know if we have plans for Friday yet."

Another eye roll, "Okay. If you can't make the meeting, then maybe we can hang out over the weekend? I kinda don't want to be alone this weekend." She lowered her eyes but not in the sad way she had earlier. This was more of a seductive look.

"Why don't you call the girl from your meeting? I heard her ask you out and give you her number. It would be good if you made some friends outside of us, Sadie. Jo and I will be here to support you through this situation with your mom, but we aren't friends in the way that you might be wanting or even needing us to be. We won't be hanging out. There won't be any talks about our relationship or sex life. Are you going to be okay with that?"

"Yeah, I'm good with that." She answered dryly and sat back in her seat.

"Great. Excuse me while I go to the ladies' room." I slid out of the booth and walked towards the back of the restaurant. I passed our waitress as she was taking our food to the table. A few minutes later, I returned, but no Sadie. There were a couple of twenties on the table, and a note was written on a napkin.

This should cover the check. Thanks for dinner, 'friend.'

Damn, I sat down and put my head in my hands.

"I don't know, babe. It sounds like Sadie was trying to work her way back into our bed. Your speech was very appropriate and needed from what you're telling me."

"Maybe, but I still feel horrible. I didn't intend to hurt her feelings, but I didn't want her getting her hopes up, thinking that was going to happen again."

"So then, like I said, you weren't wrong for what you said. You want me to call her?"

"No."

"Damn, why you gotta say it like that? You don't trust me to talk to her?"

"Oh, I absolutely trust you, baby. It's her ass that I don't trust, though so-"

"If you trust me, then it doesn't matter if you trust her or not. I'm going to call and see what her true motives are. Okay?"

"Fine."

"So you really not coming over tonight?" I slightly whined.

"No, I need to do laundry and wash my hair before my hair appointment tomorrow. Why don't you just come here?"

"Because I gotta get up early for my PT test in the morning."

"And? You can't get up early here?"

"I have to get up even earlier if I stay at your house."

"Well, I guess we'll be sleeping alone tonight then."

"It's cool. You take up the whole bed anyway."

I burst out laughing, "oh, you tried it. I'll call you back in a couple of hours when I get in bed."

"Okay, baby."

When I turned off my shower, I could hear my phone ringing in my bedroom. I wrapped one of my big towel sheets around my body and then twisted my hair up into a towel turban before walking across the floor and into my bedroom. I picked up my phone from the nightstand and saw I had two missed calls from Samantha and an 'urgent' text.

"Hey, Samantha, what's up?"

"Are you with Jo?" She asked feverishly.

"No, I'm home, and she should be at her place."

"I need you to go to her. It's an emergency."

"What happened?" My heart dropped along with my towel. I quickly found something to throw on.

"Rose called me, and apparently, there was an accident with Brandy. I don't know all of the details yet, but I want to make sure Jo isn't alone when she finds out."

"An accident? Is she okay?" I grabbed a ponytail holder and my purse as I ran out of my bedroom and down the stairs.

"No, she's not."

"Oh my... Okay, I'm on the way to her now. Don't call her until I let you know that I'm there."

"I think me and Rose are going to head over there too. Rose doesn't want to tell her over the phone."

"Okay, I'll see you guys soon." I hung up the phone and pulled out of my driveway.

"Hey Google, call Jo!" I yelled at my phone.

"Hey, babe. You in the bed already?"

"No, I decided to stay with you after all. I just wanted to make sure you were home."

"Mmmm, you just wanna lay up on me all night. Yeah, I'm here," she laughed.

"Something like that. I'll see you soon." I tried to sound as light as I could so she didn't suspect anything.

I made it to her house in record time. I sent Samantha a quick text before I got out of the car.

"Babe, where you at?!" I yelled as I walked in through the garage door.

"I'm in the bedroom! I'll be back down in a second!"

I sat my purse down on the coffee table and went into the kitchen to make a drink. I'm not sure if it would be for her or me, but I knew at least one of us was going to need it. A few minutes later, Jo bounced in the kitchen, hyper and sexy as usual.

"Hey, baby." She kissed me on the lips and swiped the drink out of my hand. "You shouldn't have." She laughed.

"I didn't." I reached around her trying to grab it back.

"Shhh, my phone is ringing." She playfully danced out of my reach before answering, "Hey, G'ma War..." Jo's face got serious in a matter of seconds, and it clicked in my head that it must be Bran's grandma, Ms. Warren.

I instinctively moved closer to her.

"Wait, what hospital is she at? I'll come get you and we… she what? That's impossible. She can't be…" Jo dropped into one of the chairs at her kitchen table, and her phone dropped to the floor. I could hear Ms. Warren crying on the phone, and then the doorbell rang. I ran to answer the door for Samantha and Rose. I didn't wait to greet them but instead ran back to the kitchen to Jo, where she was sitting in shock. Ms. Warren must have hung up because the phone was silent.

I kneeled in front of her, "baby? What did Ms. Warren say? What's wrong with Bran?"

"She's gone."

"Hey. What's going on?" Samantha asked.

"She's gone." Jo repeated with silent tears flowing down her cheeks.

"Did she say what happened?" I rubbed her legs, attempting to comfort her.

"She was in a high-speed chase with a couple of Texas Rangers. They said she cut across four lanes of traffic and in front of an 18-wheeler trying to get off the highway. She cleared the truck and hit another car and the median. Her car flipped in the air, throwing her through the windshield. She died instantly." Rose answered my question.

Jo looked up as if she were noticing that Rose and Samantha were there for the first time.

"What are you doing here?" She asked Rose.

"Jo, as soon as Rose found out about Bran, we came by so she could tell you in person and make sure you were okay."

"Why would I be okay? My best friend is dead. She's gone and...just get out. All of you... just get out." Jo got up from her chair and tiptoed out of the kitchen and up the stairs. We all jumped a little when a door slammed a few minutes later.

"You guys should go. Sam, I'll text or call you with an update on how she's doing." I wiped the tears that I didn't realize had fallen. Sam grabbed me and gave me a tight hug.

"Don't leave her. She can be really stubborn, but I know she needs you right now. If she gets too crazy, call Charlie. She knows how to calm her down even better than me."

"I'll keep that in mind, but I know how to handle her, and I am not going anywhere." I hugged her back.

"Erica, please tell Jo how sorry I am. Let me know if there's anything I can do. This is not how I wanted things to end." Rose hugged me before she walked out, and I could see a look of confusion cross Samantha's face.

"Thanks, Rose, and I know. I'll make sure she knows it too." I offered a small smile to them both and watched them holding hands down the walkway to Rose's car before closing the front door. I took a deep breath and jogged up the stairs to Jo's bedroom. She was lying across the bed in the dark, but I could tell from the way she was breathing that she wasn't asleep.

"Baby, can I get you anything?"

"No. When I said everyone, I meant you too. I just want to be alone." She didn't move from where she was lying at all.

"You can be alone in your room if that's what you want, but I'm not leaving. I'll be in the guest room if you need me." I closed the door before she could respond.

At some point in the middle of the night, I felt her get in bed with me and snuggle against my body. In the morning, I slid out of bed without waking her to call my assistant. I informed him I would be working from home for the next couple of days and instructed him to move any important meetings I had to virtual. I tiptoed back upstairs to find Jo already awake. She was sitting on the side of the bed on the phone.

"Please call me when you have the body and not Ms. Warren. No, all arrangements are to be approved by me. I will have the legal documents over to you today. Yes, a week from Friday is fine for the service. Price is not an issue—no insurance policy. I'll be paying cash. Just send me the bill once you have the price for everything. Thank you." She hung up her phone. "Good morning, baby." She greeted me, standing in the doorway.

"Good morning, love. What can I help with?" I sat next to her on the bed.

"I'm going to see G'ma in a couple of hours. I would like it if you came with me."

"Of course. Are you hungry? I can fix something or go pick up-"

"No, I'm fine. I will probably make a smoothie in a little while. Thank you."

"You're welcome."

"Thank you for staying last night. I...I don't-" Jo started to get choked up.

"Hey, no need to thank me. Whatever you need, I'm here. I've arranged my schedule so that I can work from here. I got you just like I know you got me. Okay?"

Jo nodded yes, and I leaned in to give her a quick kiss followed by a long hug. "Why don't you go take a hot shower, and I'll make your smoothie? I have a meeting in thirty minutes, but I'll be ready to go any time after that."

"I have to call Tre first. She doesn't know yet. On our way to G'ma's, I have to drop off the Health Care Power of Attorney at the funeral home. It names me as the person responsible for healthcare decisions and her funeral."

"Okay, babe. I'm free the rest of the day so we can do whatever you need to do. I'll leave you to make your call. Let me know if you need anything." I got up from the bed to head downstairs, and Jo grabbed my hand to stop me.

"I love you, woman."

"I love you more, Jo."

23. CHARLOTTE

"Good morning Doc." I greeted the doctor when she came into the room where Michael and I were waiting.

"Good morning Charlotte, Michael." She smiled at us both. "How are things with my favorite expecting parents?"

"Great!" I answered quickly in case Michael was thinking of saying something different. He just nodded in agreement.

"Good! Any concerns?"

"Not really. I've been more tired than usual, but I've only had morning sickness a couple of times. Other than that, it's been pretty good."

"Michael, you're awfully quiet this morning. Are you still in shock?" The doctor chuckled.

I squinted my eyes at him in a warning that I knew he wouldn't heed.

"I'm just a little concerned that Charlie has put herself on some limitations of sorts. I know we still have a good way to go with the pregnancy, but is there anything to be concerned about?"

"Hmm, what kind of limitations?" Dr. Fuller looked between the both of us for an answer.

"Nothing major. I've lightened my workload, and I've mostly been staying off my feet. I'm just cautious, Dr. Fuller." I rolled my eyes at Michael.

"I see. There's nothing wrong with being cautious, but I don't want you to stop living your life. I know you are normally pretty active. Why don't we see what baby Ingram has going on before we finish this conversation?" She pulled the ultrasound machine close to the bed. A few seconds later, we could hear our baby's heartbeat. Michael immediately came and stood by my side and held my hand.

"The baby's heartbeat is strong, and he or she is growing normally. Wait…" She paused, moving the wand around on my stomach to see different angles.

"Is everything okay?" Michael asked as I held my breath.

"I should say so, you're having twins!"

"What?!" We asked in unison.

"Look, there are two heartbeats. Congratulations!"

"Twins?" Michael's voice was barely above a whisper, and my strong, handsome husband had tears in his eyes.

Dr. Fuller printed an ultrasound picture and pushed the machine back to the corner of the room. "Charlotte, I know you are scared, but there is no need for you to change your whole life. You are healthy and active; I don't want you to stop doing the things you love. If we need to get to a point where you need bed rest or anything of that nature, we will discuss it. Okay?"

I took a shaky breath and squeezed Michael's hand, "okay."

"Okay. I will see you back here in four weeks. Same rules apply. If you have any spotting, pain, or if anything feels abnormal, I want you to call my office immediately. Now you two get out of here and enjoy the rest of your day together." Dr. Fuller smiled at us before walking out of the exam room.

"We're having twins?" Michael was still whispering.

"Yes, we're having twins." I smiled up at him.

"I just can't believe it, baby. I'm so happy right now."

"Happy enough to take me to lunch?"

"Anything you want, my Queen."

"Hey, Sam! What's up? I'm so excited about you guys coming to visit in a couple of weeks!"

"Hey, Charlie. I've got some bad news."

"What's wrong?" My heart sank to my stomach as I prepared for the worse.

"It's about Brandy. She died in a car accident."

"What?! Oh my! How's Jo?"

"As good as can be expected. Erica texted me an update a little while ago. She's planning and paying for the funeral for Ms. Warren."

"Ohhhh, poor Ms. Warren. This is horrible."

"It gets worse. Apparently, she was in a high-speed chase trying to escape the police when she died. I don't know all the details yet, and I'm not sure if her grandmother even knows that part."

"What? A high-speed chase? What kind of trouble had she gotten into that caused her to run from the police?"

"I'm trying to find out, and I'll keep you posted. Hopefully, I'll have an answer about that by the time you get here for the funeral."

"The funeral?"

"Yeah, I think it's in a week. I'll make sure to send you the details. I know Jo's really going to need all of us."

"Ummm, I'll call her now and talk to her about it."

"Okay, I'll talk to you soon. I love you."

"I love you too, Samantha." I looked up to Michael standing in the doorway of our bedroom.

"Everything okay? I heard you say something about a funeral."

"Brandy was killed in a car accident after leading the police on a high-speed chase."

"Wow! When is the funeral? I'll take off so we can go together."

"Not exactly sure, but it doesn't matter cause I'm not going."

"What do you mean you're not going? Charlie, Brandy was one of Jo's best friends. They've been friends since what, first grade? She just died in a tragic accident. You can't just not go."

"I know all of that, Michael, and it does not change my decision. Don't tell me what I can or can't do. I'm not going to the funeral, and that's the end of it. I'll call my sister and let her know." I slid off our four-poster bed, padded across our plush carpet into our bathroom, and slammed the door. I could hear what sounded like Michael cursing before he headed downstairs. I stared at myself in the mirror, placing my hands on my stomach.

I had a little bitty pudge that kinda looked like I had a big lunch. I'm gonna do whatever it takes to keep you two safe, I whispered to my babies.

"Hey, Charlie," Jo answered on the first ring.

"Hey, Josie. I just got off the phone with Samantha. How are you?"

"Sis, I'm really struggling. I just can't wrap my head around the fact that she's gone. Brandy had a lot of issues, but she was still like a sister to me. She's been around for most of my life."

"I know, baby. You guys have been inseparable since second grade. Oh no, Tracey! Where is she? How's she holding up?"

"I'm not really sure. She's not really speaking to me right now."

"Everyone deals with grief differently-"

"It's not that. She blames me for Bran's death." With that last sentence, Jo started crying.

"Don't cry, Jo. How can she possibly blame you for that? Sam said she was running from the police?"

"She was. Bran had gotten into some trouble, and Tre called me over so that we could talk to her.

Well, Bran didn't want to talk, so she ran. I put tracking devices in the money we keep on hand in the safes in the clubs, you know, just in case. Bran took some of the money, so I turned over the tracking information to the police so they could bring her into custody. I... I... I didn't know she would run Charlie. Why would she do that?"

"Ohhh Jo, I don't know, but you can't blame yourself for any of this. Your moral compass has always been strong. You were only trying to do what you thought was right. How could you know it would end like this? Josie, please don't take on this burden."

"I'm trying, but it's not easy. I can't help but think if I hadn't-"

"Stop it. You didn't do whatever Brandy did that got her in trouble in the first place, you didn't run instead of getting help from you and Tre, and you didn't lead the police on a high-speed chase. Brandy made those choices, Jo. You cannot take ownership of those choices. I know you loved her, but this is not on you. Tracey will come to that realization too. She's just hurting right now. Give her some time."

"You're right, and I needed that. Thank you, Charlie." Jo cleared her throat, and we sat in silence for a few minutes. "So, the funeral is next Friday at 2. I'll send you the address to the church. You probably know-"

"I'm not going to be able to make the funeral, Jo." I stopped her mid-sentence.

"Oh. Oh, okay, I shouldn't have assumed that you were-"

"Jo, I'm pregnant."

"You're what?! Oh my God, Charlie!"

"I was planning on telling you guys when you came to visit. It's not that I don't want to be there, but I'm trying to be extra careful, and I don't want to take any chances. The funeral is going to be stressful and emotional and-"

"Hey, it's okay. I completely understand. I want you and my little-"

"Nieces or nephews." I finished for her.

"What do you mean nieces or nephews? Charlie, are you having twins?!"

"Yes! I'm having twins. Can you believe it? It's too early to find out what they are yet."

"Oh, my goodness, sis! Listen, I just want you all to be safe. I know you are with me in spirit, and we'll be there to see you in person in a few weeks."

"Thank you for understanding. I know it ruins the surprise, but I had to make sure you knew the reason why I'm not there and how much I wish I could be. Please don't tell Samantha. I want to be the one to tell her."

"Of course. I'll let you handle that. Thank you for telling me. I guess I needed that too. I'm so happy for you and Michael. What did Dani say?"

"We haven't told her yet. We're trying to decide if we're going to wait until you guys come to visit so that we can tell everyone together."

"Well, if my opinion counts for anything, I think you should tell her separately. It's a big deal that she's going to be a big sister. She should have that moment with her parents all by herself."

"You know I didn't think about that. You're absolutely right. When did you become so wise?"

"Let's just say I've been working on me." Jo laughed, and it made me smile.

"Okay then. I love you, Josie, and I'm so very proud to be your big sister."

"I love you more, Charlie, and I'm proud to have you as my big sister. If you're not too busy, maybe we can visit the weekend of the funeral? Hell, if Sam and Erica can't get away, I'll come by myself."

"That would be great. Just let me know. I'll talk to you later."

"Talk to you later, sis. Bye."

Michael was on the couch in the family room watching TV. I sat next to him and leaned into his side. He put his arm around me, pulling me closer to him without breaking his concentration on whatever he was watching.

"I told Jo about the babies."

Michael turned his body toward me a little, "Really?"

"Yes. I had to let her know the reason I wasn't coming to the funeral. I didn't want her thinking it was anything else."

"What did she say? How is she holding up?"

"She's really happy for us and completely understanding. She asked if she could come down after the funeral. She said she might even come by herself. I think she just needs to get away after all this. She's holding up pretty well and hopefully a little better after our conversation."

"Well, that's good. I know how important your relationship is with your sisters, and I don't want you to ruin that. I think her coming to visit is a good idea. I'm sure she could use a big hug from you to help make it all better. When do you plan on telling Samantha?"

"I'm going to wait until she comes to visit. I asked Jo not to say anything so that she can still be surprised. Speaking of surprises, let's not wait to tell Danielle. Let's do something special with her after school tomorrow and tell her she's going to be a big sister."

"I think that's a great idea, babe. She's been asking for a family date night, so that's perfect."

"Yeah, perfect. What are we watching?" I lay my head on Michael's lap and pretended to be interested. I felt him lean to grab a throw blanket off the back of the couch and cover my body before he kissed my cheek and turned the TV down a little as my eyes drifted shut.

"Sam, would you let it go already? I told you Charlie called me and told me she wasn't able to make it to the funeral, so I'm not tripping. Look, are you coming with us tomorrow or not? Either way is fine with me."

"Wait, how are you mad at me? I'm sticking up for you!"

"I'm not mad at you, but I am tired of talking about it, and I don't need you to stick up for me." We were standing outside of the church after the repast. She had previously agreed to go to Charlie's, but since Charlie hadn't shown up for the funeral, Sam changed her mind about going. It was killing me not to tell her about the babies, but it wasn't my place, and I made a promise.

"Whatever, Josephine. If I decide to go, then I'll drive my own vehicle and meet you there." She stormed off into the parking lot.

"That didn't look good." Erica walked up next to me and slipped her hand into mine.

"Not at all." I rubbed my face with my other hand.

"I take it she's not coming with us in the morning?"

"She said she'll drive herself and meet us there IF she comes. I'm not in the mood for Sam's drama today."

"I know, babe, but she's just looking out for you. She knows how much it would have meant for Charlie to be here today."

"I told you both that I talked to Charlie, and she had a really good reason for not coming. If I'm not upset about it, then why can't everyone else leave it alone?"

"Hey, I'm on your side. If you're good, then I'm good. Did I tell you how good you look in your green and black today?"

"Actually, a couple of times. Did I tell you how good you look today?" I smiled at her. It was rare for her to wear her natural hair instead of her braids, but I loved her big natural, honey-blonde curls. They complimented her face even more so than her not quite knee-length, emerald-green dress complimented her figure. She could easily wear the dress for a night on the town, but Erica looked very classy and appropriate for a funeral with the black shawl and pearls.

"Yeah, actually a couple of times." She smiled back and leaned in to kiss me on the cheek. "I came out to tell you that Ms. Warren was ready to go, but she said she wants to ride with her neighbor."

"Who's the neighbor? Nah, never mind. I'll handle it." I spun around to go back into the church rec hall. Ms. Warren was talking to Tre, so I waited by the door until they were done. She still had barely said two words to me since I called to tell her about Bran. She sent over a check for half the cost of the funeral with a note that said, '*she was my sister too.*' I didn't feel like arguing about it, so I put it in the account Bran had set up to pay all her grandmother's expenses. Ms. Warren looked up and saw me standing by the door. She waved her hand for me to come over to them. I knew enough about G'ma War, as we called her in high school, to not even think about defying her.

"Hey, Tre. G'ma, you ready to go?"

"Josephine, I know Erica told you I was riding home with Celia. Don't come over here acting stupid."

Tre snickered a little until Ms. Warren looked over at her.

"Now, don't think I didn't notice that you two aren't speaking. I don't know what the hell y'all got going on, and I really don't give a damn. All I know is you better get it together. I done lost my last blood relative, so you two are the only family I got left. So, you get it together, ya hear me?"

"Yes, ma'am." We answered together.

"I mean it! Jo, I know you going to visit Charlie this weekend, but next weekend, I expect to see both of you for lunch on Sunday and bring Erica. I like her. Tracey, don't you bring no hoochie to my house, but if it's someone respectable, then she can come. Y'all give me some sugar 'cause Celia is waiting for me."

"Bye, G'ma." We each kissed her on a cheek before she walked off to meet her friend and neighbor, Celia.

"Jo, I'm sorry. G'ma is right. If nothing else, I have learned that life is too short. I don't want to fight with you. This has been hard enough without you."

"I feel the same way. It's been hard as hell without you, man."

"I just can't believe she's gone." Tre teared up a little, and I pulled her in for a hug.

"We gonna be alright. I'll see you next weekend but call me if you need anything in the meantime." Tre nodded in agreement. Behind her, I could see Erica and G'ma talking and hugging before she left. We ended our embrace, and I walked over to where Erica was waiting for me.

When we got to my truck in the parking lot, she reached her hand out for my keys, and I was so drained that I just handed them to her and got in on the passenger side.

"I need to go pack for Charlie's. So, we can go to my house and then go stay the night at yours if you want so you can pack." Erica said as she checked the backup camera before backing out of the parking spot.

"Nah, my bag is in the back. We can stay at your house."

"Okay, great."

I showered and got into bed while she packed her bag. By the time she came to bed, I was knocked out, but as soon as Erica got in the bed, my body instinctively was drawn to hers. I pulled her closer to me in a spoon position and nuzzled her neck.

We were up and on the road by eight the next morning. I sent Charlie a text to let her know we were on the way. I tried to call Sam and Rose but no answer. Oh well. I thought to myself.

"How did you sleep last night?" I asked Erica.

"Good. How about you?"

"One of the best nights of sleep I've had all week."

"I'm happy to hear that, baby. Are you excited you get to see Charlie?"

"Yeah, I am, but I'm really anxious to see Dani. I haven't seen my niece in forever."

"Do you think she'll remember me? It's been a couple of years since I've seen her."

"I think she will, and I know she's going to love you."

Erica smiled and put her feet on the dashboard, causing her skirt to rise up her thighs.
I cleared my throat, "you're not going to be able to ride the whole way like that."

"Why not? It's comfortable." She looked confused.

"Maybe for you, but for me, it's distracting." I glanced at her while trying to focus on the road.

"Oh really? Are you having trouble concentrating, my Luv?" She opened her legs wide and pulled her skirt up around her waist, revealing her pink lacy panties. "How about now?"

"You know you play too much, right?" I asked, only half-joking.

"Hmm, why don't you show me how much I should play?" She slipped a finger inside her panties, and I carefully slid across the highway and over to a rest stop. As soon as the truck was in park, I motioned for her to get in the backseat. Erica giggled and climbed in the back. I got out and walked to the back, locking the doors as soon as I got back inside.

"Why don't you finish the show you started?" I leaned against the door to turn towards her on the other side of the seat.

"You mean this?" Erica leaned against the other door, placed one foot on the seat and one on the floor. She pulled her skirt up around her waist again and slid a finger inside of herself. Her head fell back in ecstasy as she pleased herself.

"No, I want you to watch me, watching you."

She lifted her head and stared back at me. I knew her body so well that when her strokes slowed, and her breathing sped up, I knew she was close to climax.

"Stop," I demanded.

"Jo, I'm almost-"

"You heard me."

Erica whimpered a little and withdrew her fingers. Without breaking eye contact, I moved closer to her until I was between her legs. I slowly slid two fingers inside her, causing her to moan.

"Taste yourself."

Erica eagerly put her fingers in her mouth and licked her juice off them. I leaned down and kissed her while pumping my fingers in and out. I could tell she was already close again, so I simultaneously bit her lip and rubbed her clit with my thumb.

"Oh shit." Erica thrust her hips forward and squeezed my shoulder just as her body went stiff. A few seconds later, she had a couple of mini convulsions before her body went limp. I got a kick out watching her orgasm.

"Dammit, Jo." She mumbled, her eyes getting heavy. She always went to sleep after sex, so I covered her with my jacket and hopped out of the truck, back to the front seat. "I owe you one." I heard her say as I pulled out into traffic.

Damn, right you do. I thought to myself while also thinking how long this ride was about to be now that I was horny as hell.

"How long was I out, baby?" Erica stretched in the backseat and then climbed over the seat to the front.

"A little more than an hour. You hungry?"

"Nah, I'm good. You? Need me to take over driving?"

I chuckled a little, "no, baby, I'm straight. We only have about an hour left."

"Oooh, good. I was scared you were gonna say yeah." Erica laughed, and I playfully pushed her away.

"I should have!"

"Too late now." She was still laughing. "Still no word from Samantha? How about Rose?"

"Nope. I called them both before we left out this morning, but no answer. When I talked to Rose after the funeral last night, she said she was waiting for Sam."

"I'm glad you two are good. I thought you were going to be upset about her not coming to the funeral."

"Me and Rose? Yeah, we're straight. I mean, it's not like she and Bran knew each other like that. If anything, I thought she would have been there as a support for Sam, but that's not my business." I shrugged.

"Yeah, true. Samantha said Rose told her there was more to the case that was personal to her."

"Really? Like what?" I furrowed my brow, wondering what that could be.

"I don't know. I think they were supposed to talk last night. I'm sure one of them will tell us."

"I guess you're right." My phone rang, and my truck's Bluetooth loudly announced who it was.

"Why is Sadie calling you?" Erica asked.

"I told you I was going to call her. I forgot we were supposed to meet today. Don't make that face, woman. I told you I was going to address the situation." I hit the button on my dash to answer the phone.

"Hello," Sadie answered a little too seductively.

"Hey, Sadie. Look, I forgot we were meeting up to talk today. Erica and I are on the way out of town. If you are free, then we can meet on Monday."

"Aww, okay. I guess I can wait. Tell Erica I said hi."

"No need, I can hear you."

"Oh, hey Erica." Wow, her voice changed up real quick. I laughed in my head.

"Hey, Sadie."

"Okay, see you Monday."

"See you Monday," I said and ended the call.

Erica crossed her arms across her chest.

"Babe, don't do that."

"Do what?"

"Pout. If you insist on being there to support Sadie, then I'm going to make sure she knows we're on the same page."

"Why can't we be on the same page and go together?"

"Because I feel like I would have better control of the situation if I'm by myself. If you really don't want me to go, then I won't go, but then we just need to cut her off completely. It's your decision. Just let me know what you want to do."

"Can I think about it?"

"Of course, baby."

Erica turned up the radio, sat back in her seat, and put her left hand on my thigh. We rode in a comfortable silence the rest of the way.

Michael greeted us at the door with a big hug. He took our bags to the guest room and told us that Charlie and Dani were in the kitchen.

"Titi Jo!" Dani ran full force into me from across the room. Luckily, I knew it was coming, so I braced myself to catch her, or else we both would have ended up on the floor. After spinning her around, I put her down.

"You've gotten so big!"

"You're the same size!" We all laughed.

"Dani, do you remember Ms. Erica?"

"Yes. Titi Sam's friend. Hi Ms. Erica. Where's titi Sam?" Dani shook Erica's hand and looked around her for Samantha.

"Actually, sweetheart, Ms. Erica is here with your titi Jo. They're girlfriends." Charlie walked into the family room from the kitchen.

Dani scrunched up her face for a minute in deep thought, "can I call you titi Erica then?" She looked directly at Erica, who in turn looked at Charlie and me for guidance. We both shrugged at her.

"I would really like that." Erica finally answered, and Dani gave her a big hug. She smiled at me over Dani's head. I knew that made her day.

"Hey, my beautiful big sister." I walked over to Charlie and gave her a big hug, lingering a little longer in her embrace than usual.

"Aww, my Josie. How are you, Luv?"

"Better now." I leaned back and kissed her on the cheek.

"Me too."

"Can I?" I asked before touching her stomach.

"Yes. We told Dani last week."

I placed my hands on her stomach, "hey babies. It's your favorite titi."

Erica walked up behind me, "that is until they meet me. Oh, my goodness, Charlie, you are gorgeous and glowing. Congratulations. I guess this is as good a reason as any not to come to the funeral."

"Thank you, Erica."

I stepped back so they could hug.

"Did you guys eat yet? Dani wanted to make you pancakes, so we're cooking."

"No, we haven't eaten. Pancakes sound yummy."

Dani grabbed Erica's hand and walked with her into the kitchen.

"It looks like you've been replaced as the favorite auntie." Michael came into the room laughing.

"Yeah, yeah, yeah."

"Samantha didn't ride with you?" Charlie asked.

"I don't know if she's coming. She didn't understand why you didn't come to the funeral, and I couldn't tell her why so…" I shrugged.

"It's okay. I'll call her after breakfast."

"I don't mind not sharing you guys this weekend. It's bad enough Erica's trying to steal my favorite niece."

"I'm your only niece!"

"Okay then I won't call her. I guess we'll just see if she shows up." Charlie tried not to look disappointed, but I knew better.

"Hey, babe. How was the funeral?"

"It was really beautiful."

"You okay?"

"I think so. Jo and I just got into an argument."

"About what? You two really shouldn't be arguing, especially on a day like today."

"Can you believe Charlie didn't show up? I was fussing about it, and Jo got defensive. She said if she wasn't upset about it, then I shouldn't be either. She plays tough, but I know she was disappointed that she wasn't there."

"I know you don't want to hear this, but Jo has a point. Knowing what I know about Charlie, if she wasn't there today, then it had to be for a good reason. Either way, you gotta let Jo fight this battle if there is a battle to fight."

"Why can't you ever be on my side?"

"You know I'm not picking sides, and if I did, it would be whoever is right. The question is, why do you think you always have to be right?"

"Because I usually am."

"Okay, Samantha. Are you on the way over here?"

"No, I'm going home."

"I thought you were coming by. Do you want me to come to you? We need to talk."

"No, I'm just going to pack so we can go to Charlie's house in the morning. Are you still coming?"

"Yes, I'm happy to hear that we are still going."

"I'm not going to pass up the chance to see my niece, so yeah, I still want to go. I just pulled into my parking deck. It shouldn't take me long to pack, so I'll see you soon."

"Okay, be careful."

I watched the end of the movie I had paused when Sam called then went into the kitchen to refill my drink. I was hungry but not full meal hungry, so I started rummaging in my pantry looking for a snack. I heard Samantha struggling with her keys at the door, so I yelled out that it was open.

"It took you long enough, woman. I should have asked you to stop and get me something to eat. I'm craving something. I just don't know what."

"I can think of a few things I'm craving." A familiar voice that wasn't Samantha's said behind me. I spun around to Gloria standing in the kitchen doorway.

"Gloria? What in the hell are you doing here? How do you know where I live?"

"Hey to you too, baby. Damn, you look even better up close." Her long legs carried her across the kitchen. There was slight swelling around her right eye and a scar on her forehead, but other than that, she was beautiful and looked the same as she had in college.

"Gloria, answer my questions. What are you doing here?"

"I'm here to see you, Rose. The police told me about Bran. I can't believe you did that for me. I had lost hope for us after you called me, but you did say she would pay for what she did to me. I should have never doubted that you didn't love me."

"Did what for you? Bran died in a car accident. Are you crazy? I didn't have anything to do with her death." I backed up from her, trying to figure out what type of drugs she was on to think I had done something like that.

"Come on, baby. Don't be so modest. Let me show you how appreciative I am. I bet your tongue game is even stronger now that you've had some practice with these little hoe's. I won't hold it against you, though. Why don't you show me what you working with?"

"Why don't you explain who the hell you are and why you're throwing yourself at my woman?" Samantha bellowed from the door.

"Sam baby…"

"Oh, hi, Samantha. It's nice to finally meet you."

"I wish I could say the same. You are?"

"Samantha, this is Gloria." Sam cut daggers with her eyes at me.

"Gloria? This is Gloria?" She looked Gloria up and down before asking, "So, Gloria, I don't think you answered my question. Why are you throwing yourself at my woman?"

"I wasn't throwing anything that Rose doesn't want to catch. Besides, aren't you two just dating?" Gloria chuckled a little. "I just came by to thank Rose for taking care of the person that beat me up. I figured she would arrest her, but she went a step further, and well, I won't bore you with the details. I'm sure you know the depths this one will go to for someone she cares about. I'll call you later, Luv." Gloria kissed me square on the lips before strutting past Samantha and out the front door.

"Sam, I can explain."

"You damn well better and fast before I walk out the door and forget you are someone I care about. How could you not tell me that Brandy was Gloria's girlfriend? How long have you known? Have you two been in communication all this time?!"

"What? Baby, no, please just hear me out!"

"I'm listening."

"Jo, I'm so glad we took this little getaway to Charlie's. It was perfect!" We were on our way back to Atlanta.

"Yeah, me too, babe. Spending time with them and you was just what I needed to rejuvenate my mind and my spirit. It's been a rough couple of weeks, but I'm feeling like myself again."

"Aww, that's good, babe. I love it when you're happy."

"I love it when WE are happy. Have you decided what you want to do about the Sadie situation? I told you whatever you decide is what we will go with."

"I have, and I want you to go."

"You're sure?"

"Yes, I'm sure. I am committed to making sure she is okay if we can. Now, if after you talk to her, you think she still has ulterior motives, then... then I don't know, but our relationship comes first. I just want to give it this one last shot. Okay?"

"Okay, baby. Whatever you say. You can be the boss today." Jo laughed.

"Girl, I'm the boss every day, but okay."

Jo rolled her eyes, "Can you text her that I'll meet her at 2:00 at Papi's? That should give me enough time to drop you off at home."

I picked up her phone from the cup holder and sent Sadie a text. I barely hit send, and she was already responding.

"Looks like you're all set."

"Hey, this is only going to take a couple of hours - tops. I promise as soon as we're done, I'll come straight to you. Your place or mine?"

"I don't know yet. I'm going to the mall to do some shopping. I guess call me when you are done, and we can decide then."

"Sounds like a plan to me."

"I know you're only doing this for me, baby. I appreciate you for not thinking I'm crazy for wanting to be a part of Sadie's life. It's really important to me."

"Oh, I think you're crazy, all right, but I love how big your heart is, and I know you just want to do the right thing. I respect that."

"I'll ignore the fact that you called me crazy since you followed it by flattering words but don't let it happen again."

"Yes, ma'am."

"Babe, do you think Charlie was upset that Sam didn't show up?"

"Yeah, I know she was. She hid it very well, but I know my sister. Just like I know, Sam has good intentions, but she didn't have to take it that far. This weekend was important to all of us."

"I know. I think I'm going to call her and see if she'll go to the mall with me. See if there's something else going on with her."

"Sure pal, you do that. Let me know how that turns out."

"Nope, I'm going to keep it to myself."

"That's fine, but you know you can't keep nothing to yourself, right?"

"Oooh, that's the second insult in five minutes. You're on a roll today! Let me out of this car." We pulled up to my townhouse, and as soon as the car stopped, I swung open the passenger door.

"Hey!" Jo yelled as I hopped out.

"What?!"

"You not gonna kiss me bye?" She licked her lips and flashed her sexy smile.

"Nope."

"You gonna wish you had kissed me later. Last chance."

I walked around to the driver's side and put my hands on my hips, "if you want it, then you gotta come get it."

Jo got out, swiftly pulled me to her, and kissed me passionately, leaving me breathless as usual.

"I love you. See you soon." She kissed me on the forehead before getting back in the truck.

"I love you more."

She winked at me and drove off.

<hr>

"Jeez, what's the hold-up with the line?" I mumbled half to myself.

"Some lady is at the front talking to the cashiers. She's crying and looking for her daughter."

The girl in front of me turned around and whispered to me.

"How do you know?" I asked, standing on my tippy toes, trying to see.

"She stopped me while I was shopping and showed me her picture. Beautiful girl too. She said she thinks she works in the store."

"Oh wow, that's so sad."

A woman walked past us in the line wiping her face. Something about her looked familiar. I got out of line, put my panties on the table, and ran after her.

"Excuse me, ma'am!" I yelled. The woman sat down on a bench to compose herself, allowing me to catch up to her. "Excuse me. I heard you were looking for your daughter. Maybe I can help. I shop in this mall often." I sat down next to her.

She reached in her purse to pull out a picture, "Her name is Sadine. I've been-"

"You're Sadie's mom!"

"You know my Sadie? My God! How is she?"

"How is she?! She's devastated by the fact that you disowned her. That you wouldn't even let her say goodbye to her sister! What kind of mother turns on their child just because they are gay?! Do you know how high the suicide rates are for people in the LGBTQ community? She's going to support groups and-"

"Wait! What are you talking about? Sadie is an only child, and I didn't disown her. She's been out of the closet since she was seventeen. Her father and I always openly accepted her."

"What? But she told me… I'm confused."

"You and me both. Why don't we start from the beginning? I'm Sylvia." She extended her hand to me.

"Nice to meet you, Ms. Sylvia. I'm Erica. You want to go grab a bite to eat and get to know each other?"

"Lead the way."

We walked outside of the mall to Tin Lizzy's and asked for a patio seat. After we placed our drink and appetizer order, Sylvia started talking.

"Sadie came out her senior year in high school. I had suspected for a while, so it wasn't really a surprise to me. A mother knows these things. Anyway, a couple of years ago, she started dating this...girl. I didn't like her, and I knew she was trouble. Again, a mother knows. I also knew not to say anything to Sadie about her. One day I got a call from the hospital saying there had been an incident. Sadie tried to commit suicide. Apparently, she walked in on her girlfriend, Gloria, having sex with a guy in their apartment. After she was released from the hospital, we checked her into a mental hospital where she was diagnosed with bipolar disorder. She's fine as long as she takes her medication, but she hates taking her medication. We argued about it constantly. My husband and I came home from work, and she was gone. That was over a year ago. She changed her number and basically just disappeared. An old friend of hers from high school came by the house last night and told us she saw her working here in the mall. I just want to know that she's okay and for her to come home." Ms. Sylvia started crying just as the waitress brought our food to the table.

"Thank you. We're fine for now. Ms. Sylvia, I'm so sorry. Sadie and I have been, umm, friends for about five months now. A couple of weeks ago, she called me crying. She said she had just come out to you, and you basically threw her out without letting her say goodbye to her little sister. She said she didn't really have any other family or friends here. I've even been going with her to support meetings."

"But why? She has family and lots of friends here that love and support her. Why would she go to such elaborate lengths? If you were already friends, what did she have to gain from all of that?"

"Jo." It suddenly dawned on me.

"Excuse me?"

"Jo is my girlfriend. Sadie has a crush on her.

I sensed it, but I didn't want to believe it. They're actually out together right now."

"Well, if Sadie has a crush on her, then why are they out together? Without you?"

"Jo wanted to talk to her about appropriate boundaries in order for us to all remain friends."

"Oh, okay, that makes sense. Do you think you can convince Sadie to call me?"

"I can do you one better; I'll bring her to see you tomorrow."

"Oh Erica, that would be great! Wait until I tell her father. On second thought, I'm going to let him be surprised! Here, put my number in your phone, so you can call me when you're on the way."

"Yes, ma'am."

"And hey, food's on me! I can't believe I'm going to see my baby girl tomorrow!"

She was so happy, and although I shared her joy, I was a little uneasy. The fact that Sadie made up

all that just to get back in our lives was kind of scary.
I sent Jo a quick text telling her to be careful and call
me ASAP. Me and Ms. Sylvia sat together for the next
hour, talking and eating. I promised her I would call
her with a time tomorrow and text her when we were
on the way. She gave me the biggest hug after we got
up from the table. It almost made me feel better. Just
as I got to my car, Jo texted me and said she was
home and that she had a surprise for me. Finally! I
thought to myself. I shot her a text back and told her
I was on the way.

I pulled up to Jo's house and wondered why she
didn't shut the garage. That wasn't like her at all. I
entered the house that way, closing the garage door
behind me.

"Baby, where are you?" All the lights were off
downstairs, so I jogged up the stairs. I could hear
talking. She must be on the phone. I opened Jo's
bedroom door and stood there frozen as I watched
Sadie, naked, straddling Jo's lap.

"Hey, Erica. Care to join us?" Sadie looked me in the eyes boldly and laughed.

"Heeey Erica," Jo slurred without looking my way.

I entered the room, closed and locked the door behind me.

Other Books in the Series

The Other Side: Secrets

Samantha had a great but ordinary life, not complex at all. She had a good job, amazing friends and family plus a boyfriend that most women prayed for. She knew exactly what she wanted. That was until she started having dreams and feelings about someone that wasn't her boyfriend or in fact a boy at all. With the support of her twin sister, Jo, she explores her feelings and turns everybody's life upside down. Will her selfish secrets ruin the relationships of everyone around her? Come along for the ride with Samantha and her journey to The Other Side.

Subscribe for updates and other exclusive content at:

www.authorojaybarr.com

www.ingramcontent.com/pod-product-compliance
Lightning Source LLC
Chambersburg PA
CBHW021133190726
48288CB00008B/2640